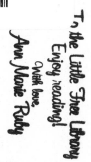

EVERMORE BELOVED:

I SHALL NEVER LET YOU GO

BOOK TWO OF THE *KASTEEL VREDERIC* SERIES

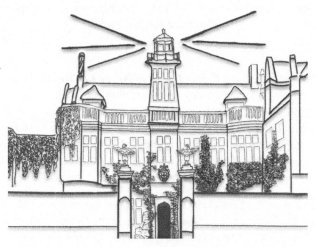

"My loving eyes seek you everywhere,
My inner sense feels you amongst all things,
My inner soul recites for you throughout time,
If only you were mine,
Evermore beloved, I shall never let you go."

Ann Marie Ruby

Disclaimer:

This book ("*Evermore Beloved: I Shall Never Let You Go*") in no way represents or endorses any religious, philosophical, political, or scientific view. It has been written in good faith for people of all cultures and beliefs. This book has been written in American English. There may be minor variations in the spelling of names and dates due to translations from Dutch, provincial languages, and regional dialects, or minor discrepancies in historical records.

This is a work of historical romance fiction framed within the true Eighty Years' War which took place in the Netherlands. Any resemblance to actual persons, living or dead, is purely coincidental. While the Netherlands, her cities, towns, and villages are real, references to historical events, real people, or real locations are used fictitiously.

Published in the United States of America, 2021.

ISBN-10: 0-578-88036-9

ISBN-13: 978-0-578-88036-5

DEDICATION

"Beloved twin flames awaken,
like the rising phoenix,
searching for one another,
placing words to the sweet song of
life,
'If Only You Were Mine.'"

Love is the magical fountain of mystical immersing caverns, where if you enter once, you are endlessly tied to one another throughout time. For even when time ends, love lives on through the given promises of the beloveds. No witchcraft or magical spells are required to tie the two hearts into one. No magical arrows can place a spell on the hearts of two beloved lovers, but their own hearts.

No one can separate true lovers from one another when their hearts beat only the other's name. Even death is shy as he separates true lovers from one another. Does death not know they are two separate individuals, yet one as they unite? Separated to be an individual they were, yet complete in union. Separating twin flames is like keeping the flute all alone on Earth, floating by itself, yet the flute player is missing. How would the flute even give us the sweet tunes if her player is missing?

This Earth is a canvas where the artist draws his portraits of life. He draws the clouds floating over a heated scorching day, to cover his beloved from the blazing heat. He draws the warm air from the skies above to cover his beloved from the blistering cold nights. Why would anyone separate an artist from his art, from his inspiration, from his love?

This world is melodious because we have love and the lovers to create with one another, a true love story. For where there is love, there is life. Where there are lovers, there is hope for the future. For where there are twin flames, there are nightingales singing and calling one another throughout the nights. For even in death, twin flames rise like the rising phoenix to begin their love stories once again.

So, today like the rising phoenix, I have brought to all of you another everlasting, eternal love story that will live on beyond time. This love story will rejuvenate your inner soul to awaken and believe in the magical spells of love. This magical shower of love is the waterfall that cleanses the inner soul of all lovers throughout time.

From this magical spell, we are gifted with musical harmony, we are gifted with magical paintings, and we are gifted with life that grows from within us. Treasure love as this is the only treasure that is not found on Earth or beyond, for it grows only within your inner soul. This can't be taken away or lost even in death, for remember through the given vows of love, you are bound to one another throughout time.

For this immortal love and the magical enchanting spells, I have woven my romance fiction as my love potion for all of you. Read this everlasting love story and learn to believe in the magical world of everlasting love once again. Hold on to the powerful words of a beloved and then may your own words be powerful to hold on to your true beloved.

I dedicate this book to all the lost lovers of life, who are still searching for their beloved twin flames. May this book be your diary to the inner heart of your twin flame. Find her or him and recite to them your everlasting love story. Jacobus van Vrederic never lost faith in his beloved as he kept writing his diary for her throughout time.

I dedicate my book *Evermore Beloved: I Shall Never Let You Go* to the seekers of true love. I have written a poem for all of you to recite to your beloved. Remember, never let them go when they are yours.

<u>IF ONLY YOU WERE MINE</u>

My magical flute does not play,

As she waits for you to play her.

My arms hug only the wind,

Pretending they are holding on to you.

Tears fall from my eyes,

Drowning all my thoughts out but yours.

My lost senses try to find your smells,

All over only to not find you.

My heart beats your name,

Only to remind me I miss your heartbeats.

My feet walk tiredly across Earth,

Only to find everyone but you.

My sweetheart, my beloved, my life, and my love,

Please know throughout time,

I shall never let you go,

IF ONLY YOU WERE MINE.

MESSAGE FROM THE AUTHOR

"The ever after bond between a founding father and the children of a nation is tied through love. This love also ties within a bond, a father and his children through his beloved from above or beyond life."

In the sixteenth century, the Netherlands was known as the Spanish Netherlands. Throughout this book, I will refer to this land as the Netherlands, to honor all lives that were lost but not forgotten as they fought for the freedom of their country. The Netherlands had finally become independent from Spain after the Eighty Years' War in 1648. During the sixteenth and seventeenth centuries, the Netherlands had fought for her freedom under the guidance of her Founding Father, Willem van Oranje.

The nation's Founding Father had wanted freedom for all of his children and fought until his children could have their own country, have freedom, and have liberty. The children of this nation had kept their given vows to their Founding Father as they brought independence to their country and all of her citizens. The Dutch War of Independence had lasted eighty years, and even beyond the death of the Founding Father. Yet, a promise made by the father was kept through the victory brought onto the land through the children of this nation.

In this romance fiction, I have a Dutch father, a husband, and a man with honor, fighting to keep his given vows to his child and his beloved. Death could not prevent a father and a beloved husband from keeping his vows. You will travel through his journey as he tried to find freedom for his beloved wife and all other women fighting through the war-ravaged country to prove their own innocence. Within a war, another silent war was brewing known as the brutal witch burnings.

A man with honor, dignity, and courage took upon his shoulders another given oath of his self-proclamation to never let another innocent woman fall prey to the hands of brutal predators. His journey began as he set foot to prove the innocence of innocent victims of a brutal war against accused witches. The Protestants and Catholics fought a ruthless war against one another during the Dutch War of Independence.

Within this war, another war called the fierce witch hunting was a way to earn some income for a lot of unjust humans. This was a way for both Catholics and Protestants to compete with one another for followers. The unjust witch burnings had ravaged the lives of so many innocent victims throughout the world. During the same time a country fought for her freedom and had found her independence, brutal witch hunts continued.

It is to be noted that within the whole of Europe, the Netherlands had one of the fewest episodes of witch burnings at the stakes or hangings at the gallows. People from all over Europe had fled to a very small town in the Netherlands seeking justice from unjust accusations. This historical place in the town of Oudewater is now known as Museum de Heksenwaag.

In this book, you all will see how a beloved had searched through land and water as he journeyed through a war-ravaged country and declared another war to save the innocent victims of the witch hunts. Throughout this time, he hoped to find his beloved somewhere in the midst, always whispering the last hope of faith, "If only my eyes could see you one more time, I would not close my eyes ever again."

His heart thumped for all innocent victims as he only saw his beloved and her innocent eyes upon all the innocent victims. A father, a husband, and a lover fought to keep his given oath to his family, to find justice for them. His child's last words haunted him throughout the days and nights as he only wished, "If only you were mine."

A child's vow to find her beloved father did not die even in death. Even as time leaves us by, the given oath of a child to her father travels time as does the oath of a father and a beloved which never dies even at death. This story travels through the Dutch War of Independence where the children of a Founding Father fought to keep the words given to their Founding Father. They brought independence to their land even after his death. Within this book, you will see how a determined beloved found a helping hand in his quest even from the beyond.

Who says life ends at death? For promises are kept even from the ever beyond. More powerful than death are the vows of an oath given by a beloved. Here in *Evermore Beloved*, a father and a beloved fought his own war and his given vows while traveling through his war-ravaged nation as he said, "Evermore beloved, I shall never let you go."

Do recite this poem to your evermore beloved when you find him or her.

EVERMORE BELOVED: I SHALL NEVER LET YOU GO

If only you were mine,

I shall never let you go.

If only I could touch you,

I would never be mine but forever yours.

If only our eyes would have met,

Your eyes would have seen my inner thoughts eternally.

If only my hands would have found yours,

I would have tied them in a knot forever.

If only I could have felt your heartbeats,

My heart would never stop beating evermore.

My dear beloved,

If only you were mine,

EVERMORE BELOVED:

I SHALL NEVER LET YOU GO.

TABLE OF CONTENTS

Dedication   i

Message From The Author   vi

Family Tree Of Jacobus Van Vrederic   1

The Inhabitants Of Evermore Beloved   2

Prologue   5

Chapter One: 16
Spirits Of Kasteel Vrederic

Chapter Two: 29
Arrival Of The Daring Seer

Chapter Three: 43
The Gallant Knight

Chapter Four: 65
Fortune Of The Roermond Witches

Chapter Five: 82
Woman Under The Veil

Chapter Six: 96
Defending Unjust Accusations

Chapter Seven: 110
Lost Memories

Chapter Eight: 121
A Priest, A Pastor, And A Nun

Chapter Nine: 144
Promises Kept

Conclusion: 159
Eternally Evermore Beloved

Glossary   175

About The Author   179

Books By The Author   184

FAMILY TREE OF
JACOBUS VAN VREDERIC

THE INHABITANTS OF EVERMORE BELOVED

All the characters in this book have typical Dutch names as they are all inhabitants of the Netherlands.

Jacobus van Vrederic — Owner of Kasteel Vrederic, Protestant preacher, husband of Margriete van Wijck, father of Griet van Jacobus, grandfather of Margriete "Rietje" Jacobus Peters, and the diarist of the *I Shall Never Let You Go* diaries

Margriete van Wijck — Beloved wife of Jacobus van Vrederic, mother of Griet van Jacobus, and grandmother of Margriete "Rietje" Jacobus Peters

Theunis Peters — Honorable soldier, husband of Griet van Jacobus, father of Margriete "Rietje" Jacobus Peters, and son-in-law of Jacobus van Vrederic and Margriete van Wijck

Griet van Jacobus — Daughter of Jacobus van Vrederic and Margriete van Wijck, wife of Theunis Peters, and mother of Margriete "Rietje" Jacobus Peters

Margriete "Rietje" Jacobus Peters — Granddaughter of Jacobus van Vrederic and Margriete van

	Wijck, and daughter of Theunis Peters and Griet van Jacobus
Bertelmeeus van der Berg	Caretaker of Kasteel Vrederic and non-blood related uncle of Jacobus van Vrederic
Aunt Marinda	Spiritual seer and twin sister of late Aunt Agatha
Sir Krijn van der Bijl	Knight, brother of Nicolaas van der Bijl, and great-granduncle of Sir Alexander van der Bijl
Nicolaas van der Bijl	Lighthouse keeper, brother of Sir Krijn van der Bijl, and husband of Emma de Vries
Emma de Vries	Wife of Nicolaas van der Bijl
Beerendeken te Bouwman	Farmer from Roermond and husband of Wilhelmina te Lindert
Wilhelmina te Lindert	Wife of Beerendeken te Bouwman
Father Adrian Jansen	Catholic priest
Pastor Willem Aertsen	Protestant pastor
Sister Blandina Maria van Straaten	Catholic nun
Sir Alexander van der Bijl	Great-grandnephew of Sir Krijn van der Bijl

Aunt Agatha	Late Catholic nun, twin sister of Aunt Marinda, and teacher of Jacobus van Vrederic, from Book One in the *Kasteel Vrederic* series
Johannes van Vrederic	Late father of Jacobus van Vrederic, from Book One in the *Kasteel Vrederic* series

PROLOGUE

"Eternal love story written in a diary signed with the tears of a beloved brings the pages back to life as she too whispers, 'If only you were mine.'"

Jacobus van Vrederic, in his private study, where he writes his beloved diaries.

Fall of 1594. I am Jacobus van Vrederic, owner of Kasteel Vrederic. I welcome all of you to the open pages of my diary. Here within the bound pages of my diary, I have gathered torn pages of my memories. Tear-filled pages, where you shall find my teardrops as my signature on all the pages. These are her tears within my eyes as a very sweet harmonious voice had sung her sweet love songs within my ears, ever so melodiously, years ago.

Her lips touched my ears as she had sung, "Your eyes, my tears."

Always I had repeated to her, "My beloved, they are your eyes, my tears."

The reason behind this was we could feel one another's pain. If she was in pain, I could feel it, while if I was in pain then she too felt it. The singer of the beautiful song, my beloved, had left me with a broken heart as her heart beats no more. Yet she never explained to me, why this heart of mine only beats her name.

This diary of mine has with ink and tears, her name written all over the pages. Even though this world says she is no more, I still hold on to this diary as her gift, to be given to only my beloved's last living image, when we meet again.

Beholder of my mind, body, and soul, this private diary too shall be shared with you to be given to our last symbol of love. I hope you don't mind as I have shared our everblooming love story with this world through the tear-filled pages of my diary. It will eventually be alive within the little hands of our last living heritor.

Your love story is written through my eyes, as it is you who had said, my eyes, your tears. So, these are my words yet your songs. Written for you through my eyes, your thoughts and mine are combined into one story, our love story.

A very cloudy autumn night. The rain started to fall very gently outside. The sounds are not sharp or gentle. The musical concert outside created by Mother Nature is calming. There is no thunder or lightning. Just the soothing sound of autumn rain pouring on top of dry fallen leaves.

Years ago, on a very cloudy winter night, I had danced within the embrace of my beloved. A couple's dance as entwined, evermore, beloved lovebirds sang the sweet song of love to one another. A burning night of passion was framed within the inner souls of twin flames, where we had burned within the inner passion for one another. The sweet passionate night had forever burned her candles of flame as we had made passionate love.

Within this magical night, I had my beloved as the only warmth and comfort, as I became her beloved and she became my everlasting love. Within her inner depth, I found my infinite love. Within the embrace of one another, we became one. Two bodies, two minds, and two souls united evermore as we became one body, one mind, and one soul, as we promised each other to one another.

Our sweet fragranced vows of two lovers tied us eternally. A vow with only words meant nothing to this world yet became our only world. Nothing but words tied us eternally together in a knot. We repeated our vows and sang to one another, "Eternally beloved, I shall never let you go."

My love if you ever come back to me, I would only say, I never want to exist without you. I want to be lost within you. For within you, I shall always be, as within me, you are forever mine.

Today my beloved, I had gone to my favorite garden where the symbol of our love lies eternally in a deep sleep with her beloved by her side. She was blessed through the eternal love of her beloved as he never let her go. To his last breath, he kept his promise. He laid eternally asleep next to her as she had laid to sleep waiting for him. Within one another's embrace they are, not afraid of the beyond, as they are together for better or worse.

I went with our sweet-fragranced bundle of joy, the last gift they had left for a cold-hearted soul to warm up by. Your namesake, my everblooming gift, from our daughter and her twin flame. You know her even from far away, as you are still so close to her through your forever motherly bond. As she is your mirror image with her looks and her soft-spoken words, in her eyes, I see you. She is our symbol of love, our precious granddaughter.

She picked flowers from the sweet divine garden of memories and laid them by her parents' bedside as she repeated with her gentle little voice of a two-year-old and said, "Forget me not, I am little Rietje."

It is her preferred name. She even calls herself, little Rietje, derived from your name and our daughter Griet's name. Her full name is Margriete Jacobus Peters. "Margriete" as she knows is her grandmother.

I held her to my chest. A cold man's heart became warm as I knew your heart still beats within my chest through her little one. I told our beloved granddaughter, "I shall never let you go."

It is then I took another vow, a lover's vow, a father's vow, and a husband's vow. I shall search all over this Earth and beyond to find you my beloved. How could you not be alive? As long as this heart beats, how could your heart not beat?

I shall never let you or your memories go. I shall find you Margriete van Wijck, and until my last breath, I shall search only for you. For these eyes don't stop pouring like the rainfall outside. For how can they stop falling as you had said they are my eyes yet your tears? So, my belief is you are out there somewhere, pouring your tears out and pulling me toward you.

Like a gentle breeze, you pull on to me. Like sweet musical notes, you pull me toward you. I shall find you and bring you back to our home. Within the inner house of my chest, you shall always be. Your permanent home is within my chest.

How is it my heart still beats your name? Then how is it your heart does not beat my name? If I am alive, then you too must be alive for I don't believe in this world and all the worldly people who say your heart beats no more. For is it not two souls and two minds and two bodies had become one, through our union? Then how is it I see you not, yet I hear you repeat evermore, "Forget me not"?

A promise I make to you my beloved is if this heart beats, then it only beats for you. As long as there is life in this body, it only lives for you. This body, mind, and soul are only yours, and I shall bring you back to me, through life or death. You shall be only mine, as I am only yours.

My beloved, I wish upon the stars far away to hold on to you evermore throughout time. I recall you had said, all the pain be yours and all the joy be mine. Today, I wish all the sorrows of life and all the joys of life be ours together in union. I only hope this life gives us the same path. May we travel upon the same path, hand in hand, in life or in death.

Wherever you are, you are mine, only mine, and I shall go above and beyond this life to be only yours. Throughout time and tide, I will search for you, until we hold hands in life or in death. May you always lay upon my chest, in life or in death.

Our daughter shall always be upon my chest through our granddaughter who is the air I breathe. Life has gifted this hard soul, with a hard gift as our daughter's lifeless body was brought back to me. I held on to our granddaughter and knew through her, I am forever bonded to our child. The air you and I had together inhaled, had dried off my tears for her. I planted the forget-me-nots at her final resting place as my symbol of love shall never let either one of you go.

When my time comes, I want to rest in the *Evermore Beloved* garden, the eternally blessed resting place, holding on to you. Through time and tide, I will unite with you in life or in death. Remember my oath, an oath of a noble Dutchman, who repeats all day and all night, "Evermore beloved, I shall never let you go."

Before I take you all on a journey to witness my everlasting love story through the pages of my diary, I want you all to read my beloved's love poem. Her poems are my lifeline through the remaining days of my life. They shall also be a glimpse of hope for all of you nonbelievers of true love stories. I hope my eternal love story grows evermore within all of your inner souls for then you too shall plant forget-me-nots to remember all love stories throughout time.

Here is my beloved's love poem which she had written as a love letter where forever she wanted to live within my eyes. She had said my eyes carried only her tears even though I promised I too shall carry all her pain, so they are her eyes and my tears.

<u>YOUR EYES, MY TEARS</u>

Heavenly rain poured upon Earth and ocean.

Earth finally kissed the ocean water.

My tears emptied nonstop,

Yet my pain never touched anyone.

Eternity passed by,

Yet my eyes never hurt from all the pouring tears.

I desired for my twin flame,

Life after life.

I crossed ocean after ocean,

As I found myself awakened in foreign lands

And different times.

Yet my eyes never hurt,

Even though my soul's moaning sounds,

Heartened all even in Heaven above.

I sought my beloved upon Earth and Heaven,

As I watched him pursuing me.

His pain-filled cries reached my soul,

As I realized my pain-filled cries,

Had reached his.

I asked him endlessly,

As I have spilled my tears,

Hoping he would find me,

In the love's reflecting weeping lakes.

I asked him but why did I not feel the tears?

He answered all my questions,

For he said,

YOUR EYES, MY TEARS.

CHAPTER ONE:

SPIRITS OF KASTEEL VREDERIC

"Heartbeats halt and the physiques are no more, yet the souls do not leave their beloved ones. They become guiding spirits, like lanterns guiding the living to finish the unfinished business left behind."

Jacobus van Vrederic in his private bedchamber with his granddaughter Rietje who is holding on to her favorite food item, bread, while his spirit son-in-law Theunis Peters watches over them.

asteel Vrederic, Naarden, the Netherlands, the first day of autumn in September of 1594. The chilly autumn morning was always welcoming to my inner soul. Neither cold nor warm yet so comfortable.

The colorful trees would be bare soon after their magical display of colors. They would bid their farewell to this Earth, as we would wait for new colorful blossoms this coming spring. Now I would just enjoy the color change as a gift for my poetic soul. A self-proclaimed poet I became, as my fingers found poetry and words to bring life back to a lifeless body.

For my beloved Margriete, I had become a romantic poet. Physically separated from you, I had become a desolate poet. I could see my small petite Margriete walking into my lonely life with her long brown hair blowing in the wind. Her fair, pale white skin glowing under the warm sun. Her smell was like wildflower fields blooming in the open air to bring joy within all lives she touched.

The cold Kasteel Vrederic had blocked off all the sounds pouring into her walls, yet this bundle of joy filled these lonely cold walls with all the musical sounds of life. The love of my life, my little Rietje, my granddaughter, my beloved daughter's last symbol, and my beloved Margriete's mirror image, bundled me up in joy. Warm and cozy on a cold winter's day and filled with blissful breeze on a hot summer's day as she kissed this Opa's cheeks with her sweet blubbers.

This was rejuvenation for a body who lived soulless, as my soul was tied and encircled with my lost love. My little darling became my rejuvenating renewal to a physical body that must keep going and restitution for a mind that must keep stable. All she had to do was look into my eyes with her big innocent eyes and say, "Opa."

My whole life froze as I forgot I even existed, and my life began with my bundle of joy. Now for you, my Rietje, my little Margriete, I would live my life. The heavy doors started to creak as the candles were flickering once again. I heard the household help start to scream once again, "Spirits!"

My eyes refused to sleep yet my soul wanted to go back to sleep to see her one more time. Like a fog, she would come and call me as if she needed my help. My beloved called me through my dreams, but where did she call me from? I wanted the dark and dingy castle doors to hide my emotions inside the room as I struggled to hide my emotions inside myself.

Again, he was back, just sitting on my chair and leisurely reading my personal diaries. A six-foot-tall, well-built man with fair skin and long blond hair with blue eyes was just watching over me. I knew this was not my mind playing games on me. Yet I wondered, how could a person I buried myself be back sitting in my room, just reading my personal diaries without any worry?

Theunis Peters, an honorable soldier who fought bravely for the Spaniards yet was honorable to the Dutch resistance fighters, fell madly in love with my daughter. For the last two years, there were spirit sightings in Kasteel Vrederic. I had so many household members quit because they all thought my castle was haunted.

One of the few staff members remaining was the eldest household member, an evergreen bachelor, Bertelmeeus van der Berg, whom I referred to as my uncle. A chubby, bald, and tall man who barely spoke unless it was on his term and his way. The only person he would talk to was my granddaughter whom he called baby Rietje.

Bertelmeeus walked into my room with my granddaughter as he said, "Jacobus, he is back again. He is now sitting at your table. You do see him, right? There are more and more sightings in the castle. Rumors are spreading as to who they were and why they are haunting the castle. Even though they have been here from the time we buried them, I don't mind but I'm worried about the other staff members who are quitting."

I did not say anything about the man whom I did see but pretended to not see.

My spirit son-in-law said, "I see you see me. Also, you have not changed. You still have brown hair and are still six feet tall. Your French beard is still trimmed."

I told him, "Why would I change as I am still amongst the living? I wish you too were still here."

He never replied and neither did Bertelmeeus. I just wanted to hold on to my two-year-old beloved granddaughter, as she waited patiently with her great-uncle whom she so sweetly called Bertelmeeus. A name she started to pronounce on her first birthday. Her first word was his name. A little shock for this Opa but it had made his life and so they became best friends for life.

I remained silent like a stone wall who could not say anything but watch the miracles that took place in front of my eyes. I loved having my daughter and her husband here as permanent residents of Kasteel Vrederic. She was the inheritor of this castle and now my beloved granddaughter is.

I stared back at my little bundle of joy, while still in bed, as she jumped up and down in excitement. She knew it was our private time to walk over to the park and play. I held on to my beloved granddaughter Rietje as I told her, "I love you, my dear. Let me listen to my sound of music, your heartbeat."

She jumped near my chest and repeated, "Opa's heart beats Rietje!"

Something inside my inner soul just poured out and landed upon my eyes. They spilled out like pouring happy raindrops. I realized she knew our sweet songs as we repeat her grandmother's phrases.

I repeated to my two-year-old Rietje, "Your heart beats my name as my heart beats your name."

I really didn't know if she grasped the entirety of the phrase, but she repeated in her heavy baby talk, "My name is Rietje and Oma's name is Margriete and Mama's name is Griet and Papa's name is Theunis and you are my beloved

Opa and the big guy is Great-Uncle Bertelmeeus, my family."

I watched her as she then watched the person standing by the study table. She did as he gestured to her. The spirit placed his finger on his lips, told her not to say his name, and blew her a kiss. She did the same gesture, placed her little fingers on her lips, and blew him a kiss.

She knew the soldier standing tall in the very corner was her father. The spirit woman who sang her to sleep and awakened her every morning with the sweet songs of her miraculous voice was her mother, my daughter. A secret she knew was only our family secret.

Bertelmeeus missed all of the exchanges as he was busy trying to feed porridge to a very busy toddler.

She screamed at him, "No more porridge! I want bread and butter with Opa!"

Bertelmeeus and I both knew a fresh basket of warm bread and fresh churned butter would be set on the dining table with fresh tea and warm milk. All of this would be placed there by the unseen spirits of the household. Yet they were very well seen by all of us who knew but didn't say anything.

Hot tea, a drink my father got used to drinking during his travels, became a favorite drink in Kasteel Vrederic. Dried tea leaves were brought back from China by my father, Johannes van Vrederic, in his early years as he had traveled with the Portuguese merchants. My father said he had seen this plant had grown wildly in India as well. To this day, we still get dried tea leaves brought back by his friends. Tea was not very well-known here yet my household had introduced themselves to this drink.

The breads were baked fresh every day by a beautiful young woman of five feet, five inches in height. She looked like her Indian grandmother, with beautiful silky olive skin, long dark black hair, and very small and petite body. She never chose sides but baked fresh bread for the soldiers of the independence war and all who needed food. It was from the bullets of the soldiers, she and her husband had passed away.

Even after her death, she still miraculously baked bread for her child and this father she never knew yet knew always from her inner soul. Even though she never entered this father's house in life, she bonded with this father through love. Her spirit became a permanent guest in her father's home. A father who had yearned to have her all of her life yet only got her after her life on Earth ended.

She is a gift from the beyond I would keep forever for she is mine. I have you my child in death and this father takes a vow, I shall never let you go. Even in death, may you be mine.

I told Bertelmeeus, "I will take my granddaughter out to the park after breakfast today."

Bertelmeeus replied, "I would advise against this as the war has gotten worse and a lot of unrest is going on. The Spaniards and the Dutch resistance fighters are fighting one another, and innocent lives are being affected. More death and unjust is going on."

He stopped and watched Theunis for a while. Then he said, "Another kind of war is going on Jacobus van Vrederic. Young maidens have been captured as they are being accused of witchcraft. I would advise to keep Rietje inside today as rumors of spirit hauntings in our castle are spreading. The dead body of Griet being intact even after days of her passing has rumors linking she might have been a witch."

He never called me by my full name, so I knew something was amiss. I had attempted to explain science to everyone, but no one wanted to learn any preservation of science or miracles from the beyond. So, I only observed everyone as the only thing I could do was allow time to take its course.

I was upset at the thought of witchcraft. It was my thought that ideas of being a witch had stopped after Charles V had witnessed the rigged witch trial in Polsbroek in 1545. He had asked all the women to be weighed at Oudewater, and if their body weight was proportional to their build on the scale, then they would be set free.

I knew all women weighed something as it was simple science and basic truth. I was irritated by the thought they were witches because they didn't weigh anything so they could fly on a broom. It was ludicrous. Women, men, and children were being burned and hung at the stakes and gallows without any fair justice. A war within a war was going on in my land.

I told Bertelmeeus, "I will have the fresh baked bread left for us by my daughter. As you know my child has gone through a hard journey to come back to her father's house, with her husband. We shall all behave in front of them and not mention this to anyone else outside of these walls. Please have the table ready for my son-in-law and daughter as they will always be members of this home."

He just watched me like he saw a ghost for the first time but said nothing as he had known about them for a while now. He only held on to Rietje and was oblivious. He was the only witness to all the occurrences of my life. He acted completely normal with them and at times you would think he loved them as much as he loved Rietje.

I watched Theunis and told him, "Come Theunis, let us all go and have something to eat as we will have Aunt Marinda over for breakfast. Hopefully, she will be able to put some light into this dark day as to why you all are here. I know you all have a greater message than what is known to all of us. I only wish you all could have told us without our asking."

Bertelmeeus only said, "I am happy! Maybe finally we will have some answers to this mystery Jacobus. I feel like we will enter an unknown dark period. Or maybe we will enter into the light, through knowledge."

I told him, "I pray Aunt Marinda can solve this mystery, and not allow a daughter's journey from the beyond to go in vain. She has come to help this father of hers, and I will try to help my child with her wishes."

In my mind, I asked Aunt Marinda to come quickly.

CHAPTER TWO:

ARRIVAL OF THE DARING SEER

"If a human mind can only grasp the knowledge that is known to him, then I ask why do we seek more knowledge?"

Breakfast buffet at Kasteel Vrederic, where Griet van Jacobus, Theunis Peters, Bertelmeeus van der Berg, and Jacobus van Vrederic make sure little Rietje always gets her fresh baked bread.

reakfast at Kasteel Vrederic was a very simple meal. Not fancy or extravagant as we were all affected by the Dutch War of Independence. Yet today, I watched Bertelmeeus had the cook make fresh hard-boiled eggs, roast mutton, fried root vegetables, pea soup, and fried battered apples with cheese and nuts. The surprise everyone had was just like every day, there on the table was left by an unknown person, a basket of warm spiced rye bread, ontbijtkoek, fresh churned butter, marmalade, fresh tea, and warm milk.

All the food served in the house had all her visitors feel this was a home where love was brewing. Kasteel Vrederic, a stone-walled castle, had growing within her fields all different flowers. Beautiful blue forget-me-nots luxuriously grew alongside wisteria vines, which made the cold castle a little more homely. Today this home would be visited by a very special guest whom everyone, visible and invisible, was expecting.

I didn't know why I had angst in my inner soul as if something big was about to happen. My feet felt like they took a thousand steps just to go to the dining hall where I had a visitor waiting for me. The very quiet castle that never talked anyway was even quieter as if it was a Pandora's box filled with hidden secrets ready to explode. The dark heavy drapes hid the outside world from the inhabitants of this castle.

A woman with gray hair and authority was walking inside Kasteel Vrederic as if she was an inhabitant of the home. I observed her from afar and knew she was in a deep meditational state or was in a deep thought of her own. No one had the courage to talk to her or ask her anything as she was seated in the dining chamber with candles burning to light the dark room even in daylight hours. All the food was neatly placed on the table as if we were ready to have a feast. Yet no one was in the room but Bertelmeeus and Aunt Marinda.

She looked up at me sitting opposite her and spoke, "Jacobus, the last time I had seen you was at your secret wedding ceremony, to the most amazingly beautiful maiden on Earth, as I believe. I had asked you to not keep this wedding a secret but all of it is in the past now."

She watched me for a long time while we started to help ourselves with breakfast. She began to talk again, "I am here to see how I can help you with the imminent battle you must confront in the very near future. As a seer, I only see what is shown to me through my dreams. Neither have I gone against the Church, nor am I a witch. You could call me a news conveyor of the future or of the past."

Little footsteps and sounds of a very active toddler grabbed all my attention. From a very stern boring person, I became a loving Opa as my granddaughter jumped onto my lap. She neither asked for permission nor did she need any. The love of my existence came in like a whirlwind and told the world there were living breathing people in this home.

I told Aunt Marinda, "This is my granddaughter. The heartbeat of this lonesome heart."

Without any permission, my little darling granddaughter spoke out loudly, "I am Opa's heartbeat, Rietje."

Aunt Marinda laughed as she came and picked up Rietje. She said, "Yes, I know. She looks like my little Margriete. The child I raised with my sister Agatha. An orphan child I had helped to bring up with my sister like our own daughter."

She looked away for a minute and was lost in her thoughts or was she looking at someone, I could not understand.

I watched her eyes travel toward where Theunis was sitting near me. He was also looking at her directly. I could see Theunis so clearly, yet I could not see my daughter clearly or at all times. I knew she was here as I could feel her presence but not see her. I wondered why. Yet I could see and hear her when she held on to my Rietje, her child.

Aunt Marinda was the twin sister of Aunt Agatha, my teacher, a Catholic nun. Aunt Marinda never became a nun as she had the power to see the future. It was a very feared talent. If others knew about her talent, they would have charged her for being a witch and a heretic.

So, Aunt Marinda stayed away from the public eye unless someone really needed her or if she had seen a future she wanted to share. She had warned me of my frightful future beforehand, yet I had not given heed and did not believe her warnings. I had referred to Agatha and Marinda as my aunts, for both had also raised me like a mother just like they had raised my beloved Margriete.

Aunt Agatha had passed away in the church fire as had my beloved and so many others. I had no clue where Aunt Marinda was all these years as she just appeared after years of being missing.

Aunt Marinda was busy feeding my granddaughter Rietje. A strange bond had taken place between a young toddler and a woman she never saw in her life. She then started to talk as if she remembered I was still in the room, as were other unseen people.

She asked, "How long have you noticed the spirits in your household? Do they speak to you or just are there, Jacobus?"

I watched her and spoke very carefully, "I think on and off for the last two years. I see one very clearly. I know there is another one who is here, but I can't see her all the time."

She told me, "So, you see your son-in-law, but you can't see your daughter always."

I was shocked and yet not shocked how she knew who they were. I knew better and did not pry on her how she knew but just watched her and told her, "Theunis Peters is my son-in-law and he is sitting next to me on the seat on my right. Yet I know my daughter Griet van Jacobus brings in the basket of bread every morning and is around here, but I can't see her all the time. I don't know why they have not moved on, and I don't want them to move on as I want to see my child one more time, not in the coffin box, but in this house. I might be selfish, but I am her father."

Aunt Marinda said, "As you know, my thoughts are just my own and are not defined by any church or belief. I have separated my views on religion and what is and what is not, unlike my sister who had walked a very fine line as a nun." She suddenly stopped as she walked to the window and tried to see through the dark heavy drapes that separated the world from viewing inside the dark house.

She said, "The outside world can't see anything happening inside of this room as the outside is separated through the dark and heavy drapery. Some humans, however, can see beyond the drapery and guide one another through their visions." She walked back to my Rietje and took her back on her lap as she sat down at the table with her cup of tea.

Aunt Marinda continued, "You can see Theunis as you had seen him or were in his company while he was here physically. You can't see your daughter always as you never saw her physically when she was on Earth. Yet she is able to come here and you do see her at times for she has left something of hers here with you. Through the tiny hands of your granddaughter, your daughter is able to come. You will

36

be able to see her if your granddaughter shows her to you at her will. Like a medium. Then you will always see her."

She watched me as I sat there not able to say anything as a preacher, which I had become for the Protestant Church by choice. I had walked all around the Netherlands trying to preach not religion but tolerance toward one another. I did not take any vows but just tried to do my civil duty as a human.

Aunt Marinda said, "The problem is in the minds of the humans not how God does what God chooses to do. God, I believe allows spirits to come back to Earth to resolve their unfinished business. Some do this through redemption or making right things that had gone wrong. Some, however, come or are allowed to come to assist the living people they left behind with some unresolved business. It is as if they had wanted to give you a message that tied them to you. Yet I believe they passed away without ever being able to tell you."

I watched her and I knew she was correct. I had done my own study and had come to the same conclusion. Yet I wondered what the unfinished business was they wanted to solve for me or share with me.

I did not have to wait as she replied, "I believe they have a message for you. They have contacted me to pass this message on to you. I bring a message from them to you through my dreams. I believe there is someone out there who needs you to rescue her and amend a broken relationship that went wrong amongst all of you. This journey will bring on more risks and more hidden secrets will be revealed. The journey won't be easy, but you must agree to this journey if you would like to resolve this situation."

I watched her in fear and thought how much more would I have to take? What more secrets are there hiding for me to uncover?

She answered my unasked question as she said, "Dear Jacobus, not all secrets are frightful as some might satisfy the unquenched thirst of the soul. You will see in the very near future. I will allow time to reveal the answers. I see but can't reveal as only time will reveal them. I will, however, guide you through the quests you must journey through. I don't keep them a secret from you by choice, but I have seen some prophecies only come true when they are not shared and are waited upon."

I asked her, "What journey are you talking about? Why is it I fear the unknown future that is to come upon my door? I only want my granddaughter to be safe and secure in this unjust world."

Aunt Marinda said, "It is your granddaughter we must protect from the unjust world and war that looms all around us. I am not speaking about the Dutch War of Independence but the other war brewing throughout Europe."

I asked her with a dreadful fear quivering within my mind as I thought don't ask and it won't be, yet I asked anyway, "What war are you talking about Aunt Marinda?"

She watched me in fear and said, "The unjust hideous crimes against the innocent women, children, and even men. The witch burnings and the witch trials of this unjust world."

She watched me and just held on to my granddaughter with her life as she spoke again, "There is a rumor spreading fast that your granddaughter is a witch, so your home has had a lot of spirit sightings. There are people who are saying you were the unwed husband who sired a child through a witch who had died but did not die as she lives somewhere out there still to this day."

I was shocked as I was not an unwed husband. I had wed my wife in the church. My beloved had died in the fire and my daughter had her daughter through her blessed wedded husband. Theunis jumped up and splattered his tea as all watched and saw a very alive-looking, handsome soldier standing in front of us. For unknown reasons, Theunis was becoming more detectable than a spirit, as was my Griet.

I watched my granddaughter call upon her mother and say, "Mama, I am Rietje and this is Opa, my heartbeat."

I saw my daughter watch her child as she too jumped up at the words of Aunt Marinda. Both were panicking and I knew they were the parents of a child this world just might unjustly accuse of being a tiny witch.

Theunis spoke very loud and clear to his daughter, "Rietje, come to Papa, and hold Mama's hand so Opa can see his daughter now."

I watched my granddaughter walk to her father and hold his hands and her mother's hands. Theunis then continued, "I would want all here to know we want your help in proving to this world our child is a normal human born from flesh and blood parents. We are guiding all of you not just for our child but other reasons we are not able to share."

For the first time, I saw my daughter standing in front of me evermore clearly, looking alive and beautiful, like an exotic princess of a father. Not just the spirit I saw floating around but like a human. Not like a clear fog but a beautiful daughter of a father whose eyes so much wanted to see his daughter.

My daughter Griet said, "Papa, we must find the knight and search for Mama. She is still alive on Earth. She needs you now as does Rietje. When you free one, you will find the other one too. Papa, I need your help. Save Mama and save your granddaughter Rietje."

She repeated, "Papa, please help Mama. I am here to guide you to her."

I could only think my beloved still breathes and knew she kept her oath, as long as I breathe, she too will breathe. I wanted to scream and break the ground I stood upon. Yet, I held my calm for my Rietje who too carries her grandmother's name and maybe the same fate, if we could not intervene.

I watched all of this as did Bertelmeeus, for all along he was a quiet observer. Now for the first time, he spoke to Aunt Marinda, "Dear sister Marinda, I have watched all of this in silence. Years ago, I had called your twin sister my

41

own sister. Today I ask you my sister to save my family from all of this war within a war. Help us. Be the candles of hope for us. Guide us through this darkness. We walk in the dark, yet you are our luminosity through your visons."

Aunt Marinda said, "Since now we can all see one another, the seen and the unseen, let us now find the knight who has more answers to our questions."

I wondered where we would find a knight whom I had never met in my life. I watched my brave soldier son-in-law and knew he was here with his wife to guide us through this situation. Just like he brought Aunt Marinda with her message, he would take us to another person on this Earth who was known as the gallant knight.

CHAPTER THREE:

THE GALLANT KNIGHT

"Dressed in weighty armor, ready to defeat your opponents, yet within your inner soul dwells a mortal heart. Bursting with human emotions, you are nonetheless the knight in shining armor."

*Griet van Jacobus is singing a lullaby to her baby
daughter Rietje and the gallant knight, Sir Krijn van der
Bijl, is humming along.*

The dark shivering night was filled with fear rather than chills as my Rietje had awakened with gripping fear. She cried and she ran with her little feet into my room. Her tears were rolling as she jumped in bed next to me. Holding on to her tightly near my heart, I saw Bertelmeeus light the lanterns and candles in the house. Candles and lanterns were not enough to comfort my dear child, so she cried her eyes out.

I held her while we walked to the windows and opened the dark heavy drapes. The moon was shining through the stained-glass windows. I told my sweetheart, "My dear heartbeat, what is it that worries you? Always let Opa have all the worries and you my heartbeat can have anything you want, even the moon."

She was a very smart two-year-old, and she said "Opa, the moon is too heavy for me to carry. I just want you, that's all. I don't want any bad man to take me away from you. I will promise to always be a good girl. I will though always want my bread and milk and never give them up because I love my bread. I promise I will be a kind girl."

I knew she had a nightmare and saw people trying to take her away. She kept on having nightmares recently and I knew they were forewarnings of the unknown future.

I told her, "No one will take you away from me, for I promise my little one, I shall never let you go, as you are mine."

My little warm princess fell asleep in my arms. I sat in my rocking chair as I rocked her all night till dawn had broken through. Bertelmeeus and two very friendly Kasteel Vrederic spirits were all sitting next to us. We knew the child was foretelling a future we must try to change at any cost.

In the autumn of 1594, the Netherlands had seen unrest from the War of Independence. The fight continued as life and livelihoods were lost in every corner. Within this time period, we were engaged in another horrifying war where the nights would be engulfed within shrieking screams of the burning witches. The burning smells did not reach the homes or hearts of the unjust but only those who had the magical sense called feelings.

I feared what the future would bring upon my door or within the little life of my beloved Rietje. Her father and mother, the spirits of Kasteel Vrederic, could watch her and only worry even more. I watched my child as she watched her daughter and spilled tears for her beloved daughter whom she could not even hold before her death.

I told them, "We will begin our journey to find the knight who has answers to our quest. After we meet him, we will continue our journey through the war-ravaged country to find more answers to our quest."

Theunis spoke and it felt like he was still here with me like our previous journey through a war-ravaged country. He said, "The witch burnings have gotten out of hand. All people care about is themselves. The rumors of Rietje being a witch are spreading around the city of Naarden. All the staff members who were here but work no more are using her as a scapegoat. Women whom you refused to marry and denied them to be a part of Kasteel Vrederic are spreading rumors as revenge."

I watched him and knew all of what he said was true. The people were all thinking my beloved wife Margriete was not my wedded wife. The rumors of an illegitimate daughter and even my granddaughter being illegitimate had spread like wildfire. I knew we must find the knight who could help prove my Margriete was not a witch and maybe was still alive fighting for her life. I did not allow my mind to wander into the thoughts of what was going on with the love of my life. I wondered about her being alone somewhere on this Earth, fighting for herself. I did not want anyone else to be haunted by my thoughts, so I let them be my secret fear within my secret soul.

The only person I lived for, or still kept my hope alive for was my beloved Margriete. For you my beloved, I still live and I shall find you as I promised. How could my heart still beat if your heart beats no more? I watched my little Rietje and knew I must keep on living for this bundle of love.

She fell asleep on top of my chest, yet it felt like my heartbeat finally stopped racing fast in fear. All I wanted to do was hold on to my little heartbeat, who knew this Opa's heart beats her name and for the person she was named after. My little baby Rietje said in her sleep, "Opa's heart beats Rietje."

Daylight brought some peace and quiet as we launched our planning. A soldier who had passed away trying to save his wife and to keep his wife's last words, had now taken the vow to save his daughter even from the beyond. My journey began as I pledged to myself, I shall originate the journey. Aunt Marinda had warned us to commence. In no way would I allow my granddaughter to be accused of being a witch.

An elderly and eloquent gentleman, six feet, eleven inches in height, entered Kasteel Vrederic. His long black hair waved in the nightly breeze, forecasting to all of his arrival. His presence had the seen and unseen residents of our home on high alert. He watched all members of the household with his ocean blue eyes, as if he was searching for someone. No one uttered a word and silence ripped through the castle.

A brave, very petite woman, who was standing by his side, broke the silence. Aunt Marinda said, "Today I have brought a very kind friend of mine who wished to see and greet you all. I will ask you all to close all the doors and windows, so no word goes outside of this room and no word from outside comes in and interrupts what we are to discuss."

I observed this newcomer as I watched my friendly spirits, Theunis and Griet, both watch him very carefully. Bertelmeeus came in with a big thump. He also had my Rietje with him. My granddaughter wanted to jump into her mother's embrace as she did most of the nights no one was watching. Her mother started to sing her favorite lullaby thinking no one was hearing except her little child.

THROUGH YOUR MAMA'S EYES

Through your Mama's eyes,

Come my baby

See this world,

Today, tomorrow,

And forever.

My dear baby,

See through your Mama's eyes,

The colorful night sky hides within her chest

Glowing lanterns as she sends them onto Earth

Like a lightning bolt to only guide you.

My revered baby,

See through your Mama's eyes,

The moon is your aunt

Who plays hide and seek

With you in the dark.

My sweet baby,

Watch through your Mama's eyes,

The stars above

Are standing guard

As they are your own knights guarding you.

My blessed baby,
See through your Mama's eyes,
The wind blows hard
So he can send you
All the flowers.

My angel baby,
Watch through your Mama's eyes,
The pouring rain is the waterfall
That quenches your thirst
Through her immortal drink.

My precious baby,
See through your Mama's eyes,
The thunder is the drum
Of musicians guiding
All to safety.

My enchanting baby,
Watch through your Mama's eyes,
The sun is your uncle
Who always greets you
At dawn.

My darling baby,

See through your Mama's eyes,

The seawater

Rises high to kiss

Your toes.

My cute baby,

See through your Mama's eyes,

The green grass grows

For you my child

So you never hurt your feet.

My loving baby,

Watch through your Mama's eyes,

The nights

Are not scary

Neither is the day.

My adorable baby,

Watch through your Mama's eyes,

All the birds are there

So they can sing sweet songs for you

Throughout the days and throughout the nights.

My cherished baby,

See through your Mama's eyes,

All your prayers will be blessed like miracles

As I shall always watch over you

And send you my immortal kisses.

My beloved baby,

See through your Mama's eyes,

This is a world where

All your dreams will be blessed and be true

As you go to sleep at night and awaken at dawn.

This lullaby

I sing for you

My treasured baby,

For remember to see this world,

THROUGH YOUR MAMA'S EYES.

The newcomer watched my little baby and went closer to her. He sat on the ground to be at her eye level. I admired the emotion he had shown my little love. It made him an admirable person within my eyes. My little baby hugged her great-uncle Bertelmeeus even more as she was scared of newcomers. Bertelmeeus too hugged his precious great-niece he raised with me, closer to his heart.

The newcomer said, "Little woman, I know I had rescued another woman about twenty-two years ago or such. She was your mirror image. She had given bread and fruits to me so many times when I had visited her in that church that burned down. How is it possible to have a child who is her mirror image?"

He watched me for a while as he said, "One stormy night, unrest broke out between the Spaniards and the Dutch resistance fighters. The brutal war had taken as her victims, innocent lives. I roamed the burnt church grounds for any sign of survivors."

He shrugged off some of his inner thoughts as he spent time looking into thin air. I knew some memories hurt more than one can handle at times. So, I just let the newcomer get a grip on his feelings.

Tea and biscuits arrived without anyone noticing on the dining table. I watched my Griet place everything on the table very quietly. I only hoped the newcomer did not notice. Aunt Marinda watched me and just smiled as if she knew what I was thinking.

The newcomer spoke, "I found a tiny little woman on the burnt grounds of the church. I knew she recently had a baby and was very weak from the childbirth, yet she was barely recognizable from the burns she suffered. She was, however, alive in my arms and she began to breathe."

I felt like the biggest loser this Earth could have had. I was so close to my beloved he was describing yet I lost myself buried in the blanket of lies weaved by the previous owner of this home. Then it registered to me, but was it my beloved Margriete or someone else? I did not have the voice to word my thoughts.

The man watched me for a while as he then said, "Her name was Margriete, and I had known her from before. As she laid close to death within my arms, she only said, 'Jacobus, forgive me. As I take my last breath, let it be in your name, but I know your heart must keep on beating even without me or my name.'"

He watched me and repeated, "She fainted within my arms. She had no clue what had happened to her or her child. She even forgot the only name she kept on whispering throughout her ordeal and painful screams of the night. Neither I, nor she knew who her Jacobus was. She had woken up a few months after this incident. I had taken her to my brother, Nicolaas van der Bijl, a lighthouse keeper who lived near the Wadden Sea with his wife Emma de Vries. My brother Nicolaas had managed the Vuurtoren Brandaris in Terschelling in Frisia. The lighthouse was ravaged by the sea. They now have a new one or are building a new one. Yet I don't know where Margriete or Nicolaas or his wife are."

I started to panic, and I knew I was shaking so much, the house too felt she was shaking with me. I watched Aunt Marinda grab a hold of me as did Theunis, my spirit son-in-law. I felt all my acquired strength of the past two decades leave my body as all I wanted to do was shout at the heavenly skies and scream how much more do I have to take.

Yet I knew I must live and breathe for my beloved's namesake. My little baby came, jerked me, and asked, "Opa okay?"

I told her, "This Opa might be made out of a rock but for you I am all tears and human who shall never leave you sweetheart."

I told the newcomer, "Please formally introduce yourself as you know who we all are, and I know we would love to be familiar with you too."

He watched me and smiled at me as he said, "I am Krijn van der Bijl. I was ordained a knight by the Holy Roman Emperor Charles V."

I remained quiet to allow his thoughts to gather in his mind. Even the cold castle who never spoke but stood witness to all the tragedies of this home was ever so silent as if even the stone manor too was waiting for a miracle to appear.

He spoke again, "I had accompanied His Imperial Majesty as he had traveled to a small village near Oudewater in 1545. As a young soldier, I had wanted to fight for my emperor more than anything else. I watched an innocent woman being accused of witchcraft and taken to be hung. His Imperial Majesty knew this was rigged and people were doing this out of greed and revenge."

I started to walk around in fear of where this topic was going. Everyone watched me as I grabbed my grandchild into my arms and cuddled her. I could place her in my chest if she could only fit.

Sir Krijn spoke, "His Imperial Majesty refused to believe the woman in front of us was lighter than one hundred pounds and would float on a broom. He had asked all women to be sent to Oudewater, to be weighed before anyone else could be sentenced to death or be accused of being a witch."

He watched my baby granddaughter for a long time as he spoke again, "The weighmaster of the Heksenwaag in Oudewater had refused to take bribes from anyone or even lie for anyone. All women would get a fair trial here, so His Imperial Majesty had given him the honor of issuing official weight certificates."

He again stopped as he sipped tea that was served for all at the table. I watched the teapot and knew I would choke if I tried to sip so peacefully like him.

Theunis started to talk aloud as he said, "How is this connected to my mother-in-law or my child? Come on man, talk! I am a soldier and even I am sweating in places I would not sweat if I was alive or in death."

Sir Krijn replied, "Margriete was your mother-in-law but she was like my child. I had sat with her and tried to heal her burns for months. As I left her with my family, I knew she would be fine, for a knight like myself must keep on working. I had taken upon my shoulders the responsibility to save as many accused witches as I could."

He helped himself with biscuits as we all realized he could see and hear the spirits of my home very clearly as he was humming the same lullaby to my granddaughter as my daughter was humming. He smiled and watched Aunt Marinda and they both laughed by themselves.

Aunt Marinda said, "Jacobus, you should know this knight is also like my brother as is the lighthouse keeper. They rescued me from the witch hunts and helped me get a certificate from Oudewater years ago. Maybe my incident will now guide us through the ordeals we must go through today."

She sat and watched everyone in silence like we all watched her as she said, "Nicolaas and his wife were accused of harboring a witch. The people around them never did believe Margriete was healed almost completely without her being a witch."

She watched me without blinking as I asked her, "Please continue."

Aunt Marinda said, "The rumor was how could a person recover from completely being burned down to ashes, without being a witch. The church was completely burned down and Margriete somehow lived. That's one of the criteria for which women are accused of being a witch."

Aunt Marinda thought to herself and remained quiet for a while. Everyone in the room impatiently watched over her yet did not want to disturb her thoughts.

Aunt Marinda continued, "Margriete had not spoken since her ordeal. No one believed she would even survive. So, Krijn and the rest of the family could not connect you to Margriete until I received a letter from a dying nun who also survived the fire. She herself had fled after she sent me the message, in fear she too would be accused of being a witch."

She sipped her tea and had a slice of ontbijtkoek, as she played with Rietje for a while. Again we all knew not to disturb a thinker when she was deep in her thoughts.

Aunt Marinda then continued from where she had stopped, "She confessed to me through her letter, she remained silent about Margriete's whereabouts in fear of her own life. Yet after twenty-two years of running and hiding for herself, she thought the least she could do is help another innocent life. She did not hide the fact about Margriete by choice but was forced by others not to link herself with Margriete. Yet the nun said she could not live with the inner guilt. So she had confessed through her given letter."

She watched me as I lost my temper and started to shout, "Where is Margriete then, and why has she not come home or gotten in touch with me? I don't believe my beloved would stay away from me without any reason. She did this once as she thought my own father would have had me killed if I had married her."

They both watched me, and Sir Krijn said, "We don't know as my brother Nicolaas and his wife were both missing after the ravaging witch hunts. Rumor has it my brother was killed. I have followed the rumors, as my men are searching for them."

He stopped for a while as he was gripped with emotion. A brave knight who is not even afraid to show his emotion is a true knight. He then said, "Margriete never said anything. She did not speak at all after the fire. We don't even know if she can speak at all or not. The woman hasn't spoken in twenty-two years. Why would she start now?"

I watched both of them as now even Bertelmeeus started to panic. He asked, "So, is my niece alive or not? Be clearer to all of us the plain people who don't understand riddles. Please say, is she alive?"

Sir Krijn, the gallant knight, watched Bertelmeeus in shock and asked, "So is Margriete related to everyone?"

I told him, "She is by heart. She never calls anyone just by name as she always relates to everyone by something. Like you too call her your daughter even though she does not know you."

Sir Krijn said, "My men secretly have sent me messages, she is again fighting for her life. I saved her once from a burning church fire and now we must save her from the unjust accusations before she is hung or burned again. I know my brother would go to any height to protect her if he were alive."

I asked him, "Where do we find her and how?"

He replied with a sigh, "So, like all the accused witches, Margriete too has been accused of witchery, because of the way she survived the fire years ago. Margriete is like a living dead who neither can defend herself nor talk for herself. My sister-in-law is trying to go to Oudewater to save her life. I heard my brother's wife is trying to take her quietly without being noticed. I just hope my sister-in-law is not caught in the middle, for she can speak for herself but she has a tendency to help all helpless women she can find along the way."

He watched all of us as he then said, "We must all be in Oudewater and hope we bump into Margriete and my family before it is too late."

Theunis impatiently stomped his feet and paced around the room in anger. My precious granddaughter Rietje too joined her father and did the same thing. Sir Krijn watched both and just smiled yet said nothing.

He continued, "I hope they reach Oudewater before anyone tries to accuse her. If we can get a hold of the messengers in between, we will. I have my group of knights and soldiers who pass on messages from one to another. During this War of Independence, there are some of us who are trying to fight another war of our own, as we are trying to save as many innocent women as we can."

I asked him, "How do we do this as our land is fighting a war for independence, to be free, and have her freedom?"

He replied, "Yes, this country is fighting for her independence. Let us pray for your Margriete and little Rietje to have a fair chance in fighting for their independence."

I watched my family while I told everyone to be prepared as we shall start our journey before dawn.

I told them, "This country will find her freedom and independence maybe in my lifetime or maybe not, but I will make sure all the women falsely accused of witchcraft or of being a witch during my lifetime, find their freedom and independence."

CHAPTER FOUR:

FORTUNE OF THE ROERMOND WITCHES

"Freedom of speech or freedom to express one's inner thoughts are basic human rights that were taken away from the mid-century witches, for how could they even have any rights when they had to prove to this unjust world, they were indeed humans?"

Jacobus van Vrederic and his group begin their journey
to save the honor of the accused witches.

A private carriage pulled by two horses carried my Rietje, Aunt Marinda, and Bertelmeeus with all the basic necessities of a little child. The rest of the group had come on horseback including Theunis and Griet who rode on horseback dressed completely in knight's attire. No one even realized they were not visible without their attire. All were complimentary from a blessed knight named Sir Krijn van der Bijl.

Our journey would be known as a missionary journey through a war-ravaged country. I was a very well-known preacher and humanitarian across the land, as Aunt Marinda was a well-known healer and a midwife. There were soldiers from Theunis's group accompanying us as our protectors through unwanted fighting that might break through.

Without any questions, they joined the group to help their beloved soldier, who they were shocked to see as a spirit yet accepted without any questions. We all preplanned Rietje would be known as Bertelmeeus's great-niece. She too knew this was a fact between the bond of the two.

Theunis spoke with his very deep and clear voice, "We were to travel to Oudewater as preplanned, yet I have from other sources been warned to be at Roermond, within a week. If we are to travel to Oudewater, we would not be able to prevent a very undesired future."

I waited for Aunt Marinda to confirm as she was sitting by a fire in a camp where we had settled very late at night.

She laughed and said, "We are blessed to have guidance from the unknown. I had seen some very disturbing dreams, yet I was told to wait till Jacobus sees something and is willing to share."

That night I had a dream. I had seen so many dreams in the last two decades where I just let my diary know the facts. It was easy to share with my diary what I could not share with the world. My dream was very foggy, where I saw a lot of women who looked like emotionless statues, walking toward the gallows ready to be hung. I tried to walk past the crowd of onlookers as I kept on hearing the shrieking cries of not statues but real fearful women.

I heard a very soft unfearful voice call out my name and say, "Remember me Jacobus. I never let you go but was taken away from you. I am a prisoner in the captivity of this world's fictitious lies of the human mind. Yet I don't know why I am left speechless. I guess I had left my mind, body, and soul with you. Now my body does not feel anything, neither pain nor joy."

I woke up screaming in the middle of the night. I would let my cold stone castle hide my screams of the night. Tonight though, in a very cold camp, I had roused all to my inner fears of the night.

I shared my dreams as I told all the truth. I told Aunt Marinda as she watched me with her huge dark eyes straight into my brown eyes. I touched my brown hair that was untidy as was my French beard, that had yet no sign of gray even though I felt like an old man.

I told everyone, "I had a nightmare where women were being taken to the gallows, to be hung. I knew some would be burned and others would be drowned, still I knew someone was being hung whom I needed to save. I heard my beloved Margriete talking to me, however, she said she could not speak or show any emotions. She told me she could only speak to me in her head, but words got lost to her as her body was frozen in time."

Aunt Marinda watched Sir Krijn as he stood up and spoke to all of us, "We must hurry to Roermond. I have it from my sources like Theunis had described, some women will be hung or burned in a few days as they were accused of being witches. The journey would be about three days or four as we also have a carriage carrying a child."

He watched baby Rietje and again said, "Our precious child will need to be taken with care, as we must make a trip to Roermond. Whoever needs rescuing we must rescue all of them and take them back to Oudewater to be weighed and saved."

Sir Krijn walked for a while as I then saw in the burning campfire, our brave and shining knight showed his age. He was in his seventies yet so very strong and resilient. I knew his experience saving so many lives was all we needed at this hour.

He said, "It will be about a four-day trip from Naarden where we still are to Roermond, at this pace. We will have to be there and then take a trip back to Oudewater which would be another three days."

Everyone heard him and I knew the campers all were thinking what our next thing should be. I told all, "I know some of you are wondering we could go faster on horseback if we split the group. Yet, I will stay with my granddaughter and take the trip with hope as fast as I can. I don't want to save one and lose the other one."

Aunt Marinda spoke, "I agree with Jacobus, we should all stay together if we have to defend one another. It is better to stay in a group. Sometimes in life, it is not the fastest route but the safest route we must think of."

Our small group consisting of Bertelmeeus, Sir Krijn, Aunt Marinda, baby Rietje, myself, and our two seen yet unseen spirits dressed in the armors of a knight all agreed to work as a group. The soldiers would come and go as they did not want to attract any attention. We agreed to travel together as a family. This life had brought us together and so this was our one family. We didn't want to separate and be lost from one another.

On a very cold yet comfortable autumn morning, we continued our journey through a war-tormented country. Our trip to Roermond from Naarden and then back to Oudewater was going to be hard with a small child. Nevertheless, we all took an oath to complete the trip.

I watched Sir Krijn pick up little Rietje and say, "Little one, today we are all trying to save you for you are so sweet and innocent, but if time lends me a hand, I know one day you will be a mighty warrior like your father and save so many more. I promise you, sweet child."

I followed Sir Krijn and Theunis as our guides. They had planned a map we would follow but always carefully so we do not grab any unnecessary attention. It was hard to think we must save innocent women, when they were victims of brutal crimes and victims of the criminal minds of their predators.

When we had started our journey, we had passed the famous Spaanse Huis, where a horrific massacre had taken the lives of seven hundred innocent inhabitants. The blood spilled in the church building placed a shiver within the inner souls of all traveling with me. History passes by us yet leaves behind the pain and chills of the horrific nights.

Time was not accounted for as days became nights and nights became days, yet we continued nonstop unless we had to stop for the safety of the baby. We had stayed in Bussum for some part of this night, as we tried to travel before sunrise, so we would not attract much attention. Theunis had taken his child in his arms very carefully as to not hurt her. I could see the emotions of a father as he held on to her. A secret of our home was being shared in front of all the travelers, as all saw spirit parents taking care of their little child.

Theunis brought the child to me and said, "We must travel through the dark and through daylight. We will enter the beautiful green Hilversum. We will continue on to the city of Utrecht and pass the famous Kasteel Duurstede before dawn, so we do not grab any attraction. If we must continue without a break, we can rest for a while late at night. I hope the baby can handle the treacherous journey."

As dusk became dawn, we traveled on through Tiel and had gotten some fruits for the baby. We passed Oss and Helmond.

Aunt Marinda had shivers as she watched Kasteel Helmond and told everyone, "This castle was burned by a fiercely raging fire. It was as if some kind of grave curse of the human creation had evolved here. I wonder if anyone like my Margriete was a victim of this castle fire. The worst part of being a seer is you see the people and their personal pain and sufferings. Sometimes it feels as though I am living in the events with them."

I couldn't totally grasp her complete feelings, yet I somehow knew what she was saying. I have lived with my Margriete throughout my entire life. Near or far, she was with me as I was always with her through our bond of eternal love.

73

The nights were easy on us as our knight was an amazing guide and leader. Sir Krijn spoke after we crossed Kasteel Helmond, "I am not worried about the night visions of the future or the past, as we must walk through life as to our best abilities. Here I am worried about my abilities of how I would save a maiden from the burning fire or being hung. I have saved many during my lifetime yet each time it gets worse. My fear is for the rescued not for I the rescuer."

He watched all of us as he said, "I don't want to place them into a ditch as I don't want an innocent to be accused because I am trying to save them. Theunis, Griet, and Marinda must take over from there as you three have an advantage we don't. As for Jacobus and myself, we will assist, but you three must lead once we arrive. Jacobus, I warn you to keep your emotions intact."

He stopped for a while as if he was gathering up his thoughts or trying to think what he should place in words and what to keep inside of him.

I told him, "Whatever you would like to say, please do say. I am not blinded by my emotions as I must protect my little Rietje and I must save my beloved Margriete with clear thinking. I need your help. So please guide."

He watched me for a while and said, "I would warn you to be ready to accept the worst and pray for the best."

He kept his face away from my eyes as to not hurt me or he did not want to share things he hid inside his inner soul. I knew he had rescued a lot of innocent accused victims from being hung or burned. I kept silent like the ever so quiet night that spoke volumes when my Margriete was in my embrace.

I watched my daughter for the first time seem very uneasy, so I asked her, "My child, what discomforts you? It seems like you are as tough as your father, yet I see at times you have so much of your mother in you. Your pacing and unease is planted so clearly within your magical eyes. Rather sweetheart, maybe it is because I am your father so I can see it or feel it so clearly."

She replied, "I am worried if our time ends on Earth, I don't know how long we would be able to go on. I want to meet my mother at least once. My heart says, I shall never let either one of you go. I know I must, but how Papa?"

I watched Griet as I knew I had no answers, yet I told her, "My child there once was a brave soldier who had told me to believe in miracles from the beyond. I had trusted him blindly. You my child have married him. So, you should believe in his words for they came true as I have had you in my life for the past two years. I searched for you in life but found you in death. Believe in miracles as they do come true."

We stayed near Kasteel Baexem and had witnessed the magical swimming pond and its amazing garden. I thought how beautiful this land was without any war or night-screeching cries that had entered even our tents at night. We wondered were they victims of the War of Independence, or were they innocent victims who were trying to flee the brutal deceitful accusers of the witch hunts?

Two nights and three days had passed so quickly we knew we must make it through this day and night. Time again was not our friend yet all we had in this formidable journey was time. We had ended at the famous historic county Horne, which was west of Roermond.

We decided to rest by the banks of the River Maas, as we were almost in Roermond. Aunt Marinda had met with some farmers and their wives as they had informed her with some unwelcome message. She introduced us to a farmer and his wife.

She said, "This is farmer Beerendeken te Bouwman, and his wife Wilhelmina te Lindert. They have helped me in the past and have waited for our arrival."

Beerendeken had said, "We have been keeping an eye out for you as we had received the message of your arrival. I will help you and your group as much as I can as Marinda had saved my very ill child, from being burned down by her accusers. Her illness was the only reason all the other farmers blamed her for their poor-producing crops. Marinda had helped us help these farmers with their harvest and then they accused us again for witchcraft even though we had tried to help them."

He stopped as he was not well and was frail and elderly. He continued and said, "Then the blessed Sir Krijn had helped my daughter to get her certificate from Oudewater and give her life back. Today we keep our daughter safely hidden away from the immoral accusers."

His wife Wilhelmina then said, "We must hurry as they have unjustly accused fifty more women, to be hung at the gallows before dawn. We must hurry and try to save as many as we can. I know some of these women are widows who were accused of witchcraft as their sickly husbands have passed away. I don't know all of them."

My heart froze as dawn was almost approaching us when we heard women screaming at the hilltop gallows nearby. As the sky above us was neither dawn nor dark, everything around us had awakened at the fearful cries of the fearful women.

Theunis jumped up as he said, "I have this uneasy feeling we must rush. There are a lot of women who are being taken to be hung in a few moments before sunrise. I tried to get into the square but somehow, I could not go there as I have never been there in my lifetime. Or maybe there is some kind of boundary or something."

Griet started to cry. She had awakened little Rietje who saw her spirit Mama cry, so she began to cry. I told all of them I will handle the situation myself.

Griet prayed, "Dear Lord, you have brought us back. It is your will not the humans'. So, let your will be and may I be able to help turn around the unjust being done by humans."

I prayed as I thought it is all about payments and greed, so I will offer them what they would not be able to refuse. I knew if I could be there in time, I would be able to buy out all the accusers and save all the women being taken to the gallows to be hung.

78

I spoke to Sir Krijn, "Would you an honorable knight accompany me to the hilltop square? There even before dawn, as the moon still shines above our heads and the sun awaits his turn to peek through the night skies, I see the gallows waiting to do yet another historical injustice. Let's go and try to pay for some innocent victims and let us set them free."

He accompanied me as did Aunt Marinda. Griet and Theunis stayed outside of the gallows area and kept a tight hold on to their baby girl as did Bertelmeeus. The farmer Beerendeken and his wife Wilhelmina stayed behind as we did not want them to get into any more trouble for trying to free witches.

The night did not want to leave us as dawn seemed so far away. My feet froze in spot as I was walking yet I felt nothing. I let the honorable knight, Sir Krijn, speak with the accusers as he handed over a small pouch to them.

They all then said, "These women are free to go except the one who is already being hung. It is too late for one such woman who can't even say her own name."

With the moon trying to bid her farewell and the sun trying to peek through, there in front of us was a woman draped in dark clothing with her head covered. The very small and petite woman bravely walked to the gallows. I don't know where I found the energy from, but I watched a spirit Griet run past me as I ran after her.

My mind, body, and soul found a magical dose of might as I found myself hold on to the very small petite woman within my arms. I held on to her as my spirit daughter had loosened the rope off of her.

I watched Theunis give Rietje to Bertelmeeus and run, as he recited the *Hail Mary*. Then he prayed, "God have mercy on me, guide me, and help me," as he too sprang into the gallows.

Griet said, "Papa, help her please."

I told her, "I have her and she is in my arms, safe and sound."

I felt and saw soft silky, brown hair touch my face as the wind blew her hair. I felt small silky hands touch my neck to grip and hold on to me. I felt a heartbeat that was beating ever so musically next to my heart.

I wanted to unveil her and see her face but could not do so without the will of the beholder. The woman fell on top of my chest as I held on to her within my chest. I fell backward and I landed on my back on the ground. The woman landed within my body safely within my arms. No movements were made nor were heard.

There were only two very strong heartbeats who sang through the fearful night. She had a veil on which covered her face. From beneath her veil, she said in a very faint whispering sound of a female voice, "Jacobus, never let me go."

CHAPTER FIVE:

WOMAN UNDER THE VEIL

"Even though she was missing during the days, the night skies prove she never left. The glorious moon shines from beneath the dark nights and she smiles and sings to all her watchers, 'I had never left.'"

Jacobus van Vrederic saves Margriete van Wijck from
the gallows without realizing she is his beloved.

awn appeared like a gust of wind. The sun finally peeked through as within my hands lay an innocent woman almost hung at the gallows. I was frozen by the whole situation, even then her uttered whispers were still playing within my ears.

The greedy people who had accused her of witchcraft had all disappeared at the sight of a small pouch filled with gulden. Fifty women were rescued today as we were able to intercede. I watched all innocent women look straight into my eyes, with river-filled tears pouring like a miraculous waterfall. They said nothing yet I felt like so much was said.

Aunt Marinda said, "Come on girls, let us all go to the farmhouse of farmer Beerendeken, nearby. We shall all have fresh bread and freshly churned butter."

I still had the very small petite woman in my arms. She was wearing a black gown with her face shielded which prevented me from seeing who was behind the veil. She fainted within my arms, calling me by my given name. I wondered was I making too much out of this? Was she just saying another person's name?

One of the women spoke, "We don't know who she is, as she never speaks. She never spoke a word in the last twenty-two years I had known her from Terschelling. I had kept her with me like my own child. I left my son and his family to save this child whom I feel so connected to. Yet she never spoke. My husband is the brother of Sir Krijn the Knight. He was killed by the accusers as he tried to save as many of us as he could."

She cried for a while when I watched Sir Krijn hold on to his breath for this was his sister-in-law, Emma. This was an elderly woman about seventy years of age whom they had mercilessly accused of witchcraft.

Emma watched us and then said, "We had come here as we were captured by a group of people who accused us of witchcraft. They killed most of our husbands and then accused us of killing them by witchery. This maiden I see like a child was only captured because she has no voice. She has not spoken since I have known her, yet she lives and breathes just like a normal person. She healed miraculously but I don't know who she is. Today is the first time I have heard her speak."

Sir Krijn stood next to me and he said, "Jacobus you should be strong as we don't know who she is, yet. If she is not your Margriete, then it will be hard on you. Until she reveals herself or allows her veil to be removed, we must be patient and wait. It is a hard journey the waiting game, yet it is our only path."

I watched everyone as we walked into farmer Beerendeken's small farmhouse. I had kept the woman in my arms. She had not even moved or uttered another word since she fell within my hands after she escaped the door of death. I held on to her ever so close to my heart, as close to my chest as possible. I did not know why I had felt overly protective about her. I guessed it was because in my heart I knew she was my Margriete. For how could my heartbeat fail to feel Margriete's heartbeats?

All I could hear was, "Jacobus, never let me go."

I could not let her go out of my arms. No one tried to take her even though we were sitting in a very small stone cottage with wood burning to keep everyone warm in the fire. I could smell fresh bread in the air.

All of the guests were given Griet's fresh baked bread that appeared always as it was needed. I watched my daughter as she was sitting next to me on a small cot waiting for the woman to awaken. I unwillingly let her go into the hands of Aunt Marinda.

I told everyone, "I shall never let her go, if only she is mine. Everyone must prove to me she is not mine before anyone takes her away from me. I will wait for her to unveil her veil. I will not stop believing."

I watched everyone stare at me like I was irrational but said nothing. I knew all of the women had wanted to wait for this unknown woman to awaken. Aunt Marinda had spent a lot of time with her as I felt the day was going nowhere and all I wanted to do was find my Margriete.

The moon was again shining above us as we did not even keep count of the days and nights that had passed by. I watched a woman walk out from the cottage with a veil on her face. She walked ever so gracefully as she saw maybe some familiar or unfamiliar faces.

Sir Krijn went to her and asked, "My dear, would you not lift your face veil for you look very similar to a person we seek? We would only know by seeing your face more clearly. We have all waited for her for years but we understand you might not be her, and it is alright as we will save as many women as we can."

She watched him and almost fainted again as I jumped up and caught her again.

She only said, "No, I only belong to Jacobus. For Jacobus, all shall end like ashes except I shall keep my love for you alive within my soul."

Her words fainted with her as her little shaky body laid fainted within my arms. All was calm and quiet as the night progressed again in the dark, except we had the glowing light of the bright moon, guiding all the lonely travelers through another very difficult night. I wanted to lift her veil and just take a look at her face if she was mine.

My heartbeat told me it was her heartbeat that I felt. They were her hands and her body that touched my own body. For I know there was no other woman on this Earth that had awakened me like my Margriete. Tonight, again, this woman had awakened my inner feelings like an outrageous lover who was lost in his emotions of the night. Like the night from years ago, I had lost all of myself to you Margriete. Within the eternal bliss of losing myself, that night I had gained all the love this world or beyond could give.

Why did I feel like this? How could I not keep a hold of my emotions? If she was not mine, then I should not have felt like this. Yet I felt like I had feelings I didn't want to share with anyone other than my Margriete. I would have to get a grip on my emotions. I had imprisoned all my emotions for so long that I could do it again.

It was easy when I controlled this for you, but it was hard when I was being intoxicated by you. I only hoped I was not drunk by your intoxicating love potion Margriete. Yet I knew how to control this attraction as you were my only temptation and for you, I could control all of my turn-ons. I felt I must find out if she was mine or else, I would help her go home and be safe as I would then move on to save my granddaughter.

Theunis spoke, "You will soon know Jacobus, just keep on believing in miracles. I understand what you are going through. I know another person who too is going through similar emotions as you, maybe a little different."

I realized my Griet, my child, the love of our union. I watched my daughter in her very spirit form as she watched over a woman, she did not know maybe was her mother or maybe was not. Yet she tended for the woman like her own mother. I knew my child had tended for people close to her and others she never even knew.

Griet asked, "Papa, is she my mother? Papa, does she even remember anything? She remembered your name so she must be Mama. Why would a woman who has not spoken for years speak, as she touches you? I believe she spoke for the first time because you jerked her memories back. She lost her memories because she probably wanted to bury the pain of losing you with her memories. I am positive she knows it is you, and that is why her memories are coming back with your touch."

I watched my daughter as I hugged my granddaughter and told both of them, "Love will be victorious always. For after everything in life or in death, love survives even time. My wedding vows I have kept as I had told Margriete, eternally beloved, I shall never let her go. Today I take another vow, if under the veil is my Margriete, then do know, evermore beloved, I shall never let you go."

The woman under the veil walked out from the cottage, then she walked to the basket of bread and helped herself with a slice. She held on to the bread and I could see from beneath her veil was a waterfall of tears. I wondered if she was Margriete and did she know these breads were gifts from her spirit daughter? She could not see me as I was sitting in the dark where neither the moon's glow nor fire from the burning logs could illuminate.

I thought how could I glow in the light when you chose to hide your moonlike glowing face from me sweetheart. For you I had taken the vow of marriage and it was for you I again had taken the vow of celibacy. No one spoke, not even the winds.

Then breaking the silence came screaming roars of a young toddler who refused to sleep in a cot without her Bertelmeeus. She screamed and said, "Bertelmeeus! Where is Opa? Where are you? I am scared. I want my bread and milk now! Mama, Papa, little Rietje is scared! Help me now!"

We all heard screams of a toddler rip the night skies as her cries could be heard loud and clear. I wondered where this tiny little child hid all those temper tantrums. I watched a mountain called Bertelmeeus run past all of us. Like an air balloon, he grabbed the tiny tot within his arms. He never stopped nor did he bump into anyone nor did anyone bump into him. We all knew when it was little Rietje, we could not keep him away from her nor could we keep her away from her great-uncle.

He said, "My baby girl, I am here and remember the promise?"

My little Rietje said with her crying voice, "I shall never let you go. But then, where were you? I am scared of the dark. I need a lantern and I need Opa right by my side."

I watched the woman in the veil walk up to the child as she said, "Griet, this is Mama. Where were you? My sweet child, we must find Papa and tell him we are still alive." She picked up little Rietje, kissed her cheeks, and held the child near her heart.

I watched my Griet break down in tears as she hugged her husband and he hugged on to her. She could not prevent being seen by all. Just like little Rietje, her mother Griet too had broken the night skies crying, within her husband's embrace. I wondered how my daughter Griet, was so much like her daughter and yet she reminded me of her mother too.

Theunis told her, "Be strong my darling and remember our vows, eternally together we are, in life or in death. Your mother will know you soon enough."

Griet cried and said, "But Theunis, that's Mama, the woman who burned herself to save me, yet today I can't even hold her. She never cared for her life as she only wanted me to be with Papa. Life is not fair and I don't know how I can stop crying."

Theunis told her, "Yes true, yet today you have given her the proof of our love. Forever she will have our bundle of love. Our baby girl is in her arms. Through this bond, we too shall be eternally with her."

They both held on to one another as I felt I had everything, yet I lost everything as I watched the proof of Margriete and my love break down in front of me. I went and tried to hold on to them as I saw both of them clearly and for the first time, I was able to actually hold on to them. I knew they were still spirits but like Rietje, I too could touch my child and Theunis.

I told them, "Life is not fair, yet I am blessed as even within this miracle I have my daughter within my arms."

I looked up at Aunt Marinda as she said, "All is the Good Lord's creating. A prayer of a mother and a father in union can break barriers and even reach the beyond. I believe in them and have seen more miracles happen."

A gust of wind came blowing into our little campfire. As the winds grew harder, the moon shined upon all even brighter. The reflecting lake near the farmer's cottage where we had camped was ever so bright with the glowing moon. All the people in the group including the rescued accused witches all prayed no one else sees this miracle or again they would be accused of witchcraft.

The woman in the veil stood up as she watched me directly. It was then the wind blew off her veil. The moon glowed upon her face and there in front of me was standing my beloved wife, my evermore beloved Margriete.

I watched her forever as all my adult life I only wanted her. Today I saw her in front of me not in a veil but uncovered from her veil looking straight into my eyes. Not a word was uttered as time had frozen in front of me. Nothing moved, not humans, not the winds. For tonight was magical and tonight the world and the heavens above had gifted me my eternally beloved.

I had taken a vow then as I stated out loud, "Evermore beloved, I shall never let you go."

Margriete watched me for a long time whilst tears spilled out of her deep as an ocean, brown eyes. She came near me and held on to my hands forever. Then she said, "Jacobus, evermore beloved, I shall never let you go."

I held on to my evermore beloved as she again fainted within my arms. In front of my eyes were the three women whom I loved evermore. My wife and my granddaughter were in my embrace as the elder one fainted holding on to the sleepy one. The third one whom I loved eternally, my daughter, stood hovering over us as she too said holding on to her husband, "I shall never let any one of you go."

This blessed night had gifted me with the biggest gift on Earth, my three women.

CHAPTER SIX:

DEFENDING UNJUST ACCUSATIONS

"Defending unjust with another session of unjust never remedies the transmuted unjust. Accusation of the unjust minds must be remedied through corrected accusations from the unjust."

Margriete van Wijck is brought to be weighed at the Heksenwaag in Oudewater in order to save her life, by her beloved husband Jacobus van Vrederic.

Howlings of frightful cries filled the night skies. Women whom we could not rescue were still being hung and burned by unjust accusers. Everywhere women were being accused of witchery as a jest, revenge, and as scapegoating.

We started to head off toward Oudewater without wasting any time. Our group had increased in size. All fifty women including my Margriete had accompanied us on our travel. Never had I thought we would have this many women to defend. I knew some of them could have gone back home, yet some of them had nowhere to go, and others were frightened to go back home in fear of being accused again.

Aunt Marinda had wanted to take all of them to safety within the blessed weighing house in Oudewater. What would happen to them afterward we never thought of, but I knew our brave knight had a plan. He only said he would let us know after we had received the certificates for all of the women.

Our journey began as Sir Krijn the Knight had stopped at the Sint-Christoffelkathedraal in Roermond. He spoke with the church minister and some nuns as did Aunt Marinda. We all stayed behind as we were instructed by our knight. Theunis went with them as he had an advantage of being there without being noticed. They all returned happy.

Theunis said, "Soon we shall have more support from the Catholic Church. It will be easier as we obtain their support."

I knew others would not say what the discussion was about, but I was glad I had my own sources. I felt a shiver within my inner soul thinking about the horse carriage and its inside residents. Three women I love the most, Margriete, Griet, and my adorable Rietje, all rode in there.

The bumps did not bother them as Margriete held on to little Rietje and Griet just watched her mother and her daughter in admiration. We had crossed the River Maas on the way, when our carriage passengers felt the jerk and I thought both Margrietes had cried out in fear. I knew Griet was calming both as she was visible to her mother and daughter.

Nevertheless, I did not know why Margriete was not talking beyond a few sentences related to us, as she once upon a time had said, "You and I is us."

I told myself, eternally I shall wait for you. You can take whatever time you need. I so wanted to tell Margriete to look at us and remember our love never died even throughout time.

Aunt Marinda said, "We have passed Horn and Baexem, yet Margriete has not gotten out which worries me if she is falling into a deep sleep. We need to awaken her and keep her awake until she is ready to talk."

I watched her concerns and told her, "We will awaken them as we are in Eindhoven. We shall spend a night here and then try to continue again."

I saw the anxiety build up on her face as she never could hide her emotions. She smiled and told me, "A good time for mother and daughter to bond. I can hear them talking though. I wonder if Griet is able to talk with her because she is her daughter or what?"

I let her talk as I often let the night talk and listen to the calls of the night. We reached Eindhoven, the city that had been burned down by troops from Gueldres in 1486. Most of this amazing city was engulfed in a huge fire in 1554. Eindhoven had been overtaken by the Spaniards and was in control of the Spanish troops, so we had to be careful not to attract any attention.

I worried for all the rescued women who had come along on arranged horseback and on feet. The battered and bruised women never complained yet smiled and seemed to be relaxed and be in peace. I realized Aunt Marinda had her ways to calm people down. Even without speaking or touching, she healed through being in peace and spreading peace.

Even though this return trip was the best journey of my entire life, the ride was hazardous and very strenuous. The walking group never stopped or complained about their physical needs. I wondered if I should say anything and knew we had Sir Krijn with us. Like a wall of comfort, I relaxed and knew I could depend on him.

Resembling a shadow, I covered her from all unwanted dangers. Like a glowing lantern, I would wait for her throughout the dark nights. We camped here for the night as I saw the women all hide within the bushes cleared by Theunis. Like always, we were supplied with fresh bread and butter. Everyone was happy and did not complain about better meals or better housing.

I watched like a glowing lantern my Margriete walk out of the carriage with little Rietje. She sat in the crowd oblivious to the surroundings as she talked with little Rietje.

She said, "My baby, don't you worry. Mama is here and I won't let anyone take you away from me. I have a letter written for your Papa in a basket if anything happens to me. Your cruel grandfather, Johannes van Vrederic, was here and he tried to prevent the fire from burning us. He apologized as he said he never knew what would happen because of his anger."

My granddaughter said, "Silly woman. Rietje heart beats only Opa, and Opa's heart beats only Rietje."

I watched Margriete as she was confused and looked into the skies ever so confused.

She started to tear up as she said, "Strange words because only Jacobus's heart beats my name, and my heart beats his name. Yes, I understand your heart could beat for Jacobus as he is your Papa, but how would you know your grandfather, you call Opa?"

Margriete then said, "My child you must tell your father, if we never meet, his father was a changed man. He loved his wife, his Indian wife, so much that when she passed away from childbirth, he never forgave Jacobus. He blamed your father Jacobus for it until he was hit by the church fire too."

She stopped as if she was thinking about something and said, "I don't know what happened to your grandfather. I had sent you with the fisherman and I guess I found you now. I can't recall much and you are too small to remember all this. I hope I find Jacobus before my time is over."

Margriete waited for a while when she stared at me and said, "You have saved my child and my life. Please send a message to my child's grandfather saying I have forgiven him. He should forgive himself and talk with his son, who he loves but I don't know why he keeps on forgetting everything. He said he forgets who he is and always thinks of revenge and his beloved dead wife. He said he hates watching any child being brought to him without a mother."

She then came over to me with Rietje and again fell asleep on my lap. I did not know if I should be angry or burst out in tears fearing this world of love.

Aunt Marinda spoke, "I had a vision of this kind yet did not want to share before I had some facts. I believe your father had memory loss. A lover who lost his wife at childbirth, he blamed you for his loss. I also think he tried to save Margriete and her child at the church fire trying to repent for his unjust. Yet when he was hurt by the fire, he forgot everything and did not allow baby Griet to enter as he had a grudge against all babies and thought they should not be separated from their mothers. For it was his thinking that is how a mother and father separate."

She watched me as I held on to my beloved in my arms. I told her, "I don't know how he felt as he had lived in a closed room solely created by himself. I would have taken away everything that had separated Margriete and me, however and whatever the difference might be. I learned to love everything as my beloved taught me love. He learned to hate everything as he taught himself to hate everything losing his beloved."

I waited and told her, "I only let my Margriete go as he had told me she became a nun and never wished to see me. I assumed she replaced our vows and retook hers, even though I had and shall keep my given vows."

After I calmed down, I told her, "My Margriete never gave up on our vows as even with or without her memories she still keeps me alive within her soul."

I asked Aunt Marinda, "How does Margriete remember some things and then just goes away somewhere else as if she is oblivious to everything?"

Aunt Marinda did not reply, but Sir Krijn the Knight told me, "She was traumatized by your loss and her child being missing. Give her time, she will be back. She is talking after twenty plus years, for the first time. My sister-in-law says she has never spoken but you must have done something. The love you two share is a miracle in itself. I salute your love story."

I watched him and thought I only want my beloved, not a love story but just my eternally evermore beloved within my chest. We had crossed the Monniksgraeve which was dug by monks. We traveled in the dark as all had rested for a while. Before dawn, we reached Vught. We had to be very careful as this was another area which had been heavily involved in war.

As daytime progressed to sunset, we had stopped at 's-Hertogenbosch. We stopped near the Roman Catholic church, Sint-Janskathedraal, and rested for a while. Again, Aunt Marinda had told us how this church too was burned down. We did not rest anywhere long enough in fear of retribution from either side of the war.

We passed by the famous Kasteel Waardenburg and we all got a lot of history lessons from Aunt Marinda. As we crossed bodies of water used for defense in the war, we walked through without anyone questioning.

I carried Margriete as Bertelmeeus had carried our little Rietje. We had finally arrived in Oudewater which was involved in the independence war. While we all felt relaxed to finally be in the only place in the whole of Europe where innocent women had some hope, the only person oblivious to all of this was my Margriete.

I had carried her by myself to the weighing house in Oudewater known as the Heksenwaag. This was the only place in the whole of Europe that gave women accused of witchery a fair trial. I had undressed Margriete myself as all her clothes had to be stripped off. They had given her a cloth which was weighed beforehand. They then removed the weight of the cloth from her weight.

Her weight was proven to be reasonable and then she got her certificate, a piece of paper proving she was not a witch. Never did she question anything as to why I had undressed her and why I was helping her but again she remained oblivious to this world.

I called Aunt Marinda to come in as she already had her certificate. I told her, "Aunt Marinda bring in my Rietje. I want her to be weighed and never want any accusation of any sort to come and hunt her even if I am alive or even when I am dead."

Margriete screamed and told me, "How could you be dead, if I am alive?"

Neither did I say anything nor did anyone as my Margriete then became silent again. My two-year-old granddaughter was brought in and had to go through the same thing. A child feared her life because some greedy person might show up and proclaim her a witch.

All the spectators watched with guilt as no one wanted to weigh a child. I asked them, "Has a child not been accused of being a witch? Have you all been so kindhearted that you let children go? Then why do I hear stories and cries of children being burned across the land?"

No one said anything as my granddaughter was quietened by her grandmother and her spirit mother who watched the ordeal yet had nothing to say. All the women we had brought with us were weighed one by one as we had all waited outside. Not a single woman was accused of being a witch. I watched the gallant knight kneel on his knees in a prayer all the while every single woman had been weighed. A brave knight kneeling and placing his head down in a prayer for innocence to prevail was in itself a triumph.

After the all-clear was given, he said aloud, "I pray not a single person, man, woman, or child be accused of witchcraft here. May this place be sacred and known as the place all falsely accused witches found peace as they proved their innocence and are able to escape the deadly punishments."

I had personally paid for all the women who had to get the piece of paper that proved their innocence. I asked our guide, the brave, kind and honorable knight, "What happens now? Are we going back home?"

He answered, "Yes, we shall all go back to Naarden, as two ministers, a Catholic priest and a Protestant pastor, both will take in all the women who have proved their innocence. A nun at Sister Agatha's convent has arranged for this to be so. All the women will be given work and training. They will be kept safely as to the convent's ability. This was a promissory vow, given to Sister Agatha before her passing away."

I thought how many lives Aunt Agatha had saved even after her death. Margriete watched me with her big brown eyes as she asked, "Where is Aunt Agatha? She had promised me she would call upon her friendly brother, the kind Sir Krijn, who would find my Jacobus for me."

She watched me for a long time as she said, "I must go and find him for he must be worried. He promised his heart beats only my name. He promised forever evermore beloved he shall never let me go. I had promised him I shall never let him go. I must find him. Please let me go, or would you help me find him?"

I watched her and told her, "I promise I shall find your Jacobus even if it is my last breath."

She touched my lips and said, "Don't say such things. Remember what I had told my love, my forever eternally beloved, if only you were mine Jacobus, I shall never let you go."

I told her, "Jacobus is yours as you are only his."

She watched me as she said, "I know I am his, but I don't know where he is. Also, how would you know my beloved and where he is? Who are you?"

CHAPTER SEVEN:

LOST MEMORIES

"Memories made between twin flames live on eternally, even when the rising phoenix, the twin flames forget their own memories."

*Theunis Peters, Griet van Jacobus, and little Rietje try
to comfort Jacobus van Vrederic as they figure out
Margriete van Wijck has memory loss.*

T he night had come with a gust of wind and pouring rains. The lightning bolts appeared, warning all creations that the roaring thunder is to come very soon. We left Oudewater and all the bad memories in the middle of the night. We all remembered and missed the brave farmer Beerendeken of Roermond. He fought against the powerful accusers to protect all falsely accused victims and became a protector of innocents as his home became eternally a shelter of protection. Even on this night, we had passed travelers who were going to the farmer's home, to seek a few nights of protection from unjust witch burnings.

Tonight, however, we were left to defend for ourselves. I assumed the very dark skies were only frightening to the eyes who feared them. I watched a very brave woman walk out under the dark skies as the rest of our group had tried to hide within the protection of something similar to parasols, made by our unseen soldier Theunis and my child Griet.

I watched Margriete and asked her, "Why are you outside? The weather is bad. Go into the tent and wait there until the storm clears."

She watched me and she tried to look into the direction of Theunis and Griet and she asked, "Why are they outside? Won't they get drenched from the rain? Also why are you getting wet in the rain? You too will get drenched."

How could I tell her I can't go and share the same tent with her and my granddaughter? For how I could control myself from not holding on to her when I know she is mine and she holds on to my mind, body, and soul? I wanted to shout to her why she does not understand she holds on to my last bit of self-control.

Then I saw her huge brown eyes and thought for only you I get tempted yet for you I will control this emotion. The woman I love more than life itself, I shall control all my feelings to only protect you my evermore beloved. I said to her, "I would only say to protect yourself, you should go and stay inside."

She told me, "Protect myself from what for I believe I must see my predators to protect myself. You should know I am scared of thunder so I must find my Jacobus, for I know all the protection in the world is only within his arms. He knows I am scared of thunder and lightning, so I know he will find me tonight."

I watched her as I saw Griet was tearing up while she held on to her husband. I prayed for my child to always have the embrace of her husband in life or in death for this lonesome night and this evermore loneliness never seemed to end. My beloved searched all over the world for me, yet did she not even know she was standing in front of me?

I was standing in front of you my love, yet you kept on saying you can't find me. I will be your shadow forever my love, and when you do remember me, I will be standing right here, waiting only for you. I know you had lost me somewhere but when you do find me, may I be in your embrace as may you be in mine.

Margriete watched me and said, "Who are you? Why is it I don't want you to leave me, yet I don't know you? Also why does my Griet call you Opa? You're not her Opa. Also how did my Griet get so old? I just had her in the church."

I watched her and thought she had so many questions in her mind, yet she was hiding under a heavy dark cloud. How could I get her out of this cloud? I watched her without a word. Shamelessly, I wanted to see her for a little while longer, so when I am away from her, I could hold on to these eyes of hers within my eyes.

She saw me for a long time and just said, "Forever my eyes became enchanted by your eyes. What kind of an enchanter are you? Why did you make me fall in love with you, yet why did you let me go? Remember our vows, if only you were mine, I shall never let you go."

Drenched in rain, she watched me and then again lost her consciousness. I caught her in my hands and told an unconscious wife of mine, "Dear beloved, I never let you go. I held on to our vows yet never did I want to break the vows of a nun. It wasn't until later I was told you too never broke our vows as you never became a nun but were protected by the kind nuns and our given promises."

The night was quiet after this incident. We had again started our travels through a very quiet cloudless night. The clear sky left all her raindrops within my eyes, as she also sent her thunder to my heart for my heartbeat became thunderous tonight. I could even feel the lightning bolts within my inner soul as I watched a very quiet Margriete hold on to a very cranky little Rietje.

Our soldier, knight, seer, and even the big Bertelmeeus all tried to calm this little toddler. Even my daughter Griet could not handle her as the child was evermore scared from the storms of the night. Even after the storm left us, the fears remained still within two hearts. I watched Oma Margriete hold on to her granddaughter Rietje and like the calm of the night, she calmed the little crying child.

Theunis came and spoke with me, "Sir Krijn said we should be back in Naarden soon. Yet I am scared what to do with both Griet and Margriete. Have you spoken with Aunt Marinda for her help? She can guide you onward."

I told him, "Yes, I have spoken with her. She has told me, Margriete is like a sleepwalker. I should not awaken her until she is ready. She warned me to keep an eye out on her always so she does not walk backward from where she is now. She is talking and that's a good sign."

Aunt Marinda overheard us as we were the ones walking today. Our group was taking turns horseback riding and walking. We did not have enough horses on our way back.

Aunt Marinda said, "We must be careful she does not get into another shock. She could remember everything and be completely normal or go backward and go back into a shock. Jacobus, you must walk very carefully, for I believe she somehow knows you. The twin flames never separate, Jacobus, even in separation they remember one another. You two are twin flames who have risen from the ashes as you reunite again for one another."

Sir Krijn came and told us, "We have reached Woerden, where even religious figures have been burned at the stakes for their heretic views. People have saved their lives by disavowing their heresies. Anyone trying to save accused witches will be burned at the stakes. So, we must exit quietly and quickly."

I realized a lot of fear had overshadowed our group. We passed Breukelen, then we passed Bussum, and then arrived in Naarden. Our trip back was very short and quick as we had all been gripped in the thought of what laid ahead, no one had said a word.

Bertelmeeus had come out on foot as he talked with me, "Jacobus, we have arrived here, and I would like to be there with both Margriete and Rietje when we enter the house. I could not protect Margriete and Griet in the past, but today I will not allow any one of my baby girls to be taken away from me. All three are my babies, including my spirit Griet. I could not have her in life, but I have her now. Please I ask you, do something so we can keep all three."

I watched him and watched Griet and Theunis watch over Bertelmeeus. Griet said, "Dear Great-Uncle, you have me eternally, I mean really I am here as is Theunis, your eternal guests."

He watched both of them and said, "Not my guests, but you are the real owners of this castle. I am your great-uncle who is destined with you through love."

Sir Krijn the Knight had come and told all of us, "I will now take my leave as I must take all the women back to the two churches for their protection. Our path will separate but not now as I will come back soon with some guests who will help us furthermore. You shall know about this as Marinda will remain with you until Margriete heals completely."

I wondered who our future guests were, yet I knew not to question an honorable knight unless he volunteered to say. I had bid farewell to all the women who had left us. I watched the glowing moon shine on my Margriete as she just stood still in front of Kasteel Vrederic.

I heard a lot of commotion as if there were a lot of people outside our castle. They must have been hiding somewhere as I could not see anyone. I walked toward the sounds, as I tried to see where the commotion was coming from.

Outside the castle before the bridge, there was an iron gate that kept Kasteel Vrederic hidden from the outside world. Then, there was a small river that twirled under the stone bridge that led to the castle grounds. A very safeguarded castle, yet I questioned how people got on top of the bridge as it was separated by the gate and protected by a small river. I assumed people make their way in when they want to.

There under the glowing moon, I heard a sudden banging sound. I wondered whether an invisible lightning bolt hit something. What was the banging sound?

All I saw and heard was Theunis running from one side as he said, "Jacobus don't you dare!"

Then I watched Sir Krijn running back from the bridge as he screamed and said, "No!"

I heard Griet scream and shout, "Papa!"

I watched Bertelmeeus say, "Jacobus get back up now!"

My baby Rietje cried, "Opa heart beats Rietje!"

That's when I watched Margriete run toward me as she screamed and said, "Jacobus don't leave me again for you said, as long as I am alive you shall never let me go. Oh my God! Jacobus promise you won't leave me! Evermore beloved, I shall never let you go."

Everything became dark.

CHAPTER EIGHT:

A PRIEST, A PASTOR, AND A NUN

"All wars divide people against one another, yet it is within wars humans find greater than their own beliefs or needs, their inner awakened humanity for which humans unite for one another."

Theunis Peters and Griet van Jacobus sit on top of a fireplace mantle as they watch over Margriete van Wijck and Sister Blandina Maria van Straaten, while asking their child Rietje not to say anything.

Tears fell on my chest as the dark drapes and the stone walls hid all the motions of the outer world outside Kasteel Vrederic. I could see my private chamber. My bedroom was exceedingly crowded with familiar faces. The pouring rain on the castle roof could be heard like a rhythm. I watched a very petite woman sleep on top of my chest as her tears covered my chest. I also felt another small woman, a two-year-old, who too was lying on top of me.

I tried to get up as I saw Theunis look over me like he was not going to move even if he was ordered. I saw my daughter Griet sitting on my chair. On my table was my very personal diary, which she was reading. I laughed as I knew the diary had said on top of it, "To Griet, my beloved daughter with all my love and blessings."

I watched Griet take a feather quill and write something on top of it. She saw me and whispered in my ears, "Love you Papa! Welcome back! I took the liberty and wrote where you had written my name, 'To my beloved daughter Rietje, with all my love and blessings, from your Mama Griet, as this was left to me from your beloved Opa.'"

I tried to get up but had two very sleepy ladies on my chest, so I blew a kiss to my daughter. Theunis was watching me for a while and said, "You scared us and almost killed us, but your plan did not work as we are already dead. Stop terrifying us. You have two beautiful women you must take care of. They sleep at the same time and both awaken at the same time. Aside from the age difference, they look identical."

He watched both women with admiration and then said, "I wish I had known them both while I was alive. One was missing and the other one was just born."

His wife came and held on to him as she said, "We are blessed to be able to have this Theunis, since this is a gift. We must finish our job and get Mama and Rietje acquainted with one another. Nonetheless, I think they found one another and have bonded very well."

I told both of them, "I pray you both are always here to guide all of the family members. For I am blessed I still have you. The two frightened women sleeping on my chest also have found one another."

I thought for a while should I ask why I was here, and why are these two sleeping on top of me? Not that I mind, I actually love having both. One is my beloved wife and the other little one is our child's last symbol of love, our precious granddaughter, my heartbeat. Once I had thought my heart only belonged to my Margriete yet this little bundle of joy had taken over my heart in a different kind of way. She also became my little heartbeat, our little Rietje.

I asked them, "What had happened?"

Theunis said, "As we were all entering the gate, there beyond the Kasteel Vrederic gate, by the jungle near the river, a lot of people had waited for us. It was hard to see as the stone wall protecting the Kasteel Vrederic ground is covered with flowers and the bridge was covered with flowering bushes, so the people were trying to blend in."

He stopped to gather his thoughts. Then he said, "Jacobus, these people came to hunt you down. They have accused you of freeing accused witches. There was a person who took a shot at your back. Yet because Griet intervened with her basket of breads and Margriete threw them at the shooter, the bullet brazed your shoulder and fortunately missed you. He said you were wrong to bring these women back to their land."

Theunis, Griet, and I both watched the two sleepy princesses, one a grown-up woman and the other one a two-year-old toddler sleeping identically holding on to me. Both had silky brown hair and the same skin tone. Even in their weird way of sleeping, they both looked very graceful. Both classy women, the adult and the toddler, snored loudly at the same pace. Within my eyes, I knew I had three women to whom my heartbeat belonged. One, I never saw in life but in death, my daughter, and the other two were my wife and my beloved granddaughter.

Theunis then said, "Sir Krijn and Aunt Marinda have both been busy as these people have started an unrest that has spread like wildfire. A group of people are coming today to help and guide our group. I will fight for my family until I have exhausted all systems out."

I thought how could I comfort my family members from the beyond who were still trying to guide all of us? I knew I must protect my family and make Kasteel Vrederic a safer and better place. We must have permanent guards outside on the bridge, that separate our home from the world.

Margriete woke up as little Rietje also broke the silence and started to cry. My toddler granddaughter jumped on top of me, giving more pain to the wound I had suffered. Yet it felt really good to see my little tot sleeping healthy and well on top of me. Then I watched the bigger Margriete do the same as she broke into tears.

She said, "Jacobus, how dare you get shot! You should have known better not to get shot! You promised me, your heart will always beat my name."

Little Rietje said, "Silly Oma! His heart only beats my name as I told you, it says Rietje."

She laughed and hugged the child as she said, "Sweetheart, now my heart too will add your name to his name in it as it will say both of your names. For him, I found my child and now for her, I found you. So, I have all of your names beating in here."

Rietje watched all the emotions of the adults and just giggled away as she thought everyone was silly. Then I watched my wife watch me like she just woke up from a deep sleep.

Margriete said, "Jacobus, how could I forget you? What happened to me? I saw the guy in the bush as he was pointing the gun at you. Without thinking, I threw the basket of bread that appeared in my hand from nowhere at him. I knew baskets after baskets had appeared from nowhere as all of us kept throwing them on the group."

She surveyed me and our daughter for a while and said, "I was in a deep sleep yet it was as if something knocked the wind out of me. I knew my husband, my child, and everyone around me. It felt as if the bullet had hit me, not you."

I watched my brave daughter and knew it was her intervention that saved my life. If only I could give up my life to save hers. I would do anything in this world to have been there when she was shot on the back, by people she had baked bread for.

She jumped up as she watched me and said, "Papa, this heart beats as long as your heart beats. You can feel my heartbeat inside my daughter's chest forever, for you are mine and from Earth or beyond, I shall never let my Papa or Mama go."

Margriete walked to Griet and said, "I wanted to ask you, who you were. You looked so familiar, as if I had known you forever, yet I didn't know you."

Griet watched her mother as tears fell from her eyes. I watched my very courteous, peaceful, and courageous daughter nibble her lips as she stood there silently not knowing what she should say or what she should not say. Her beautiful black hair blew in the air as her dark eyes became a beautiful waterfall. Her soft ever-loving nature was blessed by her mother.

Margriete held her child and said, "Black hair, olive skin, red lips, within the eyes of this mother, my daughter is the most beautiful woman on this Earth, or heavens above. I had lost my memories but not the sense of time and not the memories of a child I had held in my arms, only for a few hours. I knew Rietje was my daughter somehow, now I know how. She is my child's daughter, my baby granddaughter."

She stood there silently as she said, "I had asked your father to give me all the tears and he bear all the joy, yet he gave me a fog, a heavy cloud that could remove all of his memories from my soul, but he could only fog all of it, not remove it."

Margriete wiped the tears of her child and said, "Buried within the overcast haze, I had lived in excruciating pain of the loss, and not knowing the truth."

She watched me for a while, as we both spoke eye to eye. Forever she believed we could speak eye to eye. Without even uttering any words she would read my mind, as I read her thoughts so clearly. She just blinked and spilled tears, and I knew she read my mind as I read hers. Through the door of eternal love, we read one another clearly.

Margriete touched her daughter and said, "My love became victorious against all the obstacles combined. God did hear a mother and a beloved's prayers as today I have you and Jacobus through a phenomenon from only God."

Griet cried as she said, "I have finally found my parents whom I searched for throughout my living life. I must have had the blessings of my parents, as blessed I am to have found both of you, not in life but even after death."

Mother and daughter hugged one another. For the first time, a child and her mother stood in front of one another. A mother cared not that her child was a spirit or living as she was able to hug her child, a spirit who had traveled from the land of the dead to only be with her parents. I knew love was the only healing medicine this family needed.

Then Margriete picked up our beloved granddaughter and said, "You my little miracle shall forever be our evermore beloved."

She gave the precious child a big and long kiss, as if placing all the kisses she had missed placing on her. I watched my beloved wife and thought my dear you have so much more of that you need to give to others too. Yet I said nothing.

She watched Theunis and said, "To be with one's beloved in life or death is nothing but a miracle. I pray you both be tied together in union through life or in death. A love story that shall be recited through all the lips that sing the sweet tunes of true lovers, throughout time."

He hugged Margriete and said, "Throughout time, all lips shall recite Margriete and Jacobus as the true beloveds who never let one another go as he recited day and night, in his awakened state and his sleep, 'I shall never let you go.' I am blessed to be able to witness this chronicle."

Theunis continued, "We must all be prepared for the guests coming here tonight. They might not be able to see us, but you must take their help."

Bertelmeeus came in and took little Rietje as she jumped into his arms and started to cry. He held her in his arms near his chest and very easily calmed her down. He watched everyone as he said, "Dear Griet, I hope you did not mind as your mother had called me Uncle, I had asked little Rietje to call me Great-Uncle. I so much wanted to hear the call from your lips. I had thought if only I could hear the words from this tiny tot, it would help fill the gap I had left open for you. This little one, however, calls me lovingly by name, as it was her first word. So I give you permission to call me by the name, Great-Uncle, as always you are my baby too, like your mother and this tiny one."

I watched Griet go and kiss her great-uncle as he blushed and said, "By God, this was a miracle. I felt the kisses of my child."

He took little Rietje out of the room giving us some privacy. I saw my beloved just watch me and not say anything. I told her, "If your tears are mine and my eyes are yours then it seems like your memories and mine are forever ours."

She watched me and said, "Forever yours I was, and I am, for I never left you, but got lost within the minds of the unknown, the unjust, and the terrors of life."

Without any word or any talk, she then kissed me on my lips. She held on to me as she cried for a long time and said, "Jacobus, I hate thunder and lightning as I feel lonely and scared and lost. Never let go of me ever again."

I held on to the love of my life as I watched the two onlooking spirits. They held on to one another refusing to leave the room and give any privacy as both of them took on their hands the duty of on-the-spot nurses.

Margriete watched everyone and smiled as she said, "I just figured out I am a grandmother, so you know I have a lot of responsibilities to take care of before any more unrest. I promise as today I have my family, I will do my share to stop the unjust witch burnings that have shattered families apart like broken mirrors. No one shall take my baby Rietje away from me. No other mothers or daughters should be burned or taken away from their families Jacobus. We must win this battle against the unjust witch hunts."

This night I thought would be a romantic night as it seemed after thousands of years, I had my evermore beloved within my embrace. I said nothing as I knew we were going to start or maybe end another war that was brewing in my war-ravaged country. Instead of a very romantic night, I had a physically painful night. My wound tried to heal with the help of Aunt Marinda and her herbs that burned more than the pain, but I knew I must endure the burn to be healed.

On this night, like the pouring rain we received from above, we had some guests who came in with the rain. They were eagerly anticipated yet unfamiliar guests. As the rainfall became louder and nature was showing her fury outside, inside we had guests waiting for us in the withdrawing room. I had asked Bertelmeeus to invite them to our parlor, so our family could all face one another including the guests and everyone would feel welcome.

As I walked downstairs to our parlor, I saw there were three guests seated whom I could only see from the back. The honorable Sir Krijn was in conversation with them as was Aunt Marinda. I watched all the people had stood as I entered the room. It was still hard for me to walk whilst the pain of the bullet that brazed my shoulder still caught me.

I saw a six-foot-tall, elderly gentleman about sixty years of age, come in. I presumed from his attire, he was a Catholic priest. Then I saw there was another gentleman about five feet, ten inches tall, around the same age, yet he was identifiable as a Protestant pastor who too walked in. Then I saw a very familiar face, a very elegant nun whom I knew from my childhood. Her name was Sister Blandina Maria van Straaten from Aunt Agatha's church. She too cordially walked in. The group was seated in the parlor.

Theunis and Griet walked into the room with their child who was walking in quietly, yet she ran and grabbed on to her Oma Margriete's hand. The child was evermore entwined with her grandmother intuitively. She said, "Oma, we have guests. We must be at our uttermost good behavior in front of them."

Rietje laughed and giggled with her little hands covering her mouth. She watched her parents and knew they too watched her and placed their pointer fingers to their lips, telling her it's time to be quiet. She nodded and sat quietly.

She then watched Bertelmeeus bring in tea and biscuits for our guests. I watched our house spirits walk up and grab tea and help themselves to be seated on top of our stone fireplace, which was more than twenty feet tall. I hoped no one else saw them. I also hoped little Rietje did not ask her parents to take her up there too. Margriete smiled as she knew what I was thinking and placed the child on her lap, kissing her cheeks ever gently.

The Catholic priest said, "I am Adrian Jansen. I have been ordained a Catholic priest. Within our teachings, we are to believe in humanity first. If I go against any of the rules of the Church, then I have broken my vows, but I believe all women, men, or children hence accused or not by another person for his own greed or jealousy or to scapegoat another, does not justify any hanging or burning at the stake."

He watched the other man as the other man said, "I am a Protestant preacher like you Jacobus. My name is Willem Aertsen. I am not bound by any marriage vows or anything. I just try to preach as I believe it is a human right, we all must teach one another. Nonetheless, I too do not agree we the humans have the right to burn or hang at the stakes or gallows anyone because people have different views or opinions. Yet it seems now what all are doing is scapegoating. I must stand up and help human rights first. Our nation is battling for her freedom. How could we stand on the same ground and not allow accused witches to have a fair trial and freedom?"

Then I watched Sister Blandina as she hugged me and kissed my cheeks as I kissed her back. She said, "I have known you from when you were even younger than your granddaughter, and it hurts me to even think some people had taken a shot at you for saving lives."

Sister Blandina helped herself to hot tea that my family had imported back during our family travels. As she served others in the room, she watched my spirit daughter and son-in-law who were sitting on top of the fireplace mantle, having their tea. She smiled at them and I watched Griet wave at her as I thought I saw Sister Blandina wave back at her. Griet closed her mouth and placed her waving hand on her mouth in shock.

Sister Blandina then said, "We will all help you and your family through this hurdle as humanity overpowers the minimal differences we have. Nothing comes before humanity, for if one loves God, then one should love all humans alike."

Then Father Jansen said, "You are blessed to have a family for you were not ordained by any church nor had you taken the vow of celibacy as you tried to bring peace and spread peace around the country."

He sipped his tea for a while and then said, "I am under the vows I have taken. I know as I work with different faiths and go against witch burnings or brutal hangings because my humanity does not allow me, I might have to face inquisition. I might even be burned at the stakes for working with all faiths."

He walked nervously as Pastor Aertsen said, "I might be burned at the stakes as might Sister Blandina for all her work to fight against the witch burnings and hangings. Unjust is when we watch innocent lives taken out because of humanmade wars, against humanity."

Sister Blandina said, "The Dutch War of Independence is needed to have freedom for our land and our people, so we can live unitedly and happily with one another in peace. Still this unjust war is ravaging around the world. The witch burnings need to be stopped for the sake of humanity. I have taken a vow to save and respect all lives on Earth, not attack anyone who disagrees with me. So, I am alright with being defrocked or having an inquisition or even being hung or burned at the stakes."

Then Father Jansen said, "We all probably remember the stories of other priests being burned at the stakes in Den Haag not very long ago, but we must do our own part of humanity. Those are my human vows, aside from all other vows I have to the Church, which I shall never break as I love God far more than any humans with corrupt intentions or minds."

I told them, "I am honored by all of your courage and honesty, yet why are you all here risking your life, and how could I help you in this journey? I will do whatever I can, but I don't wish to harm or place any of your lives at risk."

Then Sir Krijn spoke, "They were the people who have taken in the women we had brought back with us. Some women have disavowed their heresies and are spending the rest of their lives in abbeys. Some are, however, staying at the churches in fear of their lives, even though they carry a certificate with them."

I knew there was much more to their story than they were letting me in. I wished to ask but knew I must allow for their thoughts to be gathered. I just wished I could do something to bring peace within my nation and all the accused witches who had suffered under brutal and unjust scapegoating.

Margriete started to talk, "I am not very shrewd nor am I able to understand what you all are trying to say, but please say honestly without hiding anything. Is Jacobus at any risk for saving all of us?"

They all watched my beautiful wife as the woman was the picturesque of all true beauty on and beyond Earth. Her words might be very soft, nevertheless, she was always very direct. Nothing stayed within her chest. If she felt it, then the feeling would come out through her words.

Sister Blandina said, "Yes, his life is at risk, however, we have all our parishioners and our townspeople onboard. We shall always protect one another. That is what we have bonded for. Through humanity for humans, we have unitedly asked all citizens in our cities to gather up and protect one another, through all the wars that we face now or tomorrow or the future."

She watched our spirit couple and said, "Even though we have rumors of hauntings around your castle, we have on very high recommendations there are no such things as even a child lives here very comfortably under the care of her grandfather."

Margriete corrected her and said, "She lives with her grandparents. If you have forgotten, my husband and I raise her with the help from her great-uncle Bertelmeeus and her great-aunt Marinda. I can assure you this home has no hauntings other than one's own mind and the games of one's inner mind."

She took a sip of her tea and said, "My child was buried near our home in a garden that symbolizes only love and beauty. She was a martyr, as the Dutch resistance fighters and the Spaniards all had courteously bid farewell to my children. I was the only one who could not attend. If you do happen to go and visit their graves, do remember to pick some forget-me-nots, for yourselves and the church, as then all of you shall be blessed. You will see your home too will be blessed by fresh baked breads. Never shall you or anyone you love go hungry."

Everyone watched little Rietje jump into her grandmother's arms as she said, "Rietje heart beats Opa and Oma. Rietje pick forget-me-not from garden called, *Evermore Beloved.*"

Sir Krijn spoke as he said, "There are no hauntings or spirits in this home as I too have resided here and with the family for a while. I know this family like my own, as Margriete might not remember, but I took her in as my own child. She is the daughter I never had yet now I have. This house will always have one spirit protecting her grounds. That's my spirit when I am no more. Until then, I shall protect her grounds from Earth. If anyone does see a ghost or spirit, then it is I, Krijn the Knight, who protects Kasteel Vrederic from even before my death."

I watched our honorable knight take a break and think to himself. I wondered what he had planned or if he was planning again for something. I knew he only drifted off when he was preplanning something in his mind.

Then Sir Krijn spoke again, "There is also help from the Leiden University as some professors have heard about Jacobus and his journey to save innocent women from burning at the stakes. They have declared they will join in the fight against unjust burnings as humanity comes first. We also have other protections we have put in place."

He watched the two spirits floating in the room. We knew we would continue to save all the women we could save from the unjust war of the witch burnings, yet tonight we just wanted peace to spread in the air.

As the evening guests had gotten up to take their leave, Father Jansen said, "At times, spirits return to help the ones they have left behind. It is very normal, as it is but ordained by the Creator just like these two. The young woman is his daughter, and the soldier is the brave son-in-law who had stood by the Kasteel Vrederic bridge to protect his father-in-law when the attack had come from all sides. I hear it was because of their intervention, lives were saved."

He stopped and watched the spirits and laughed to himself yet said nothing to the spirits of Kasteel Vrederic. I heard him talk within his group again very loudly. I had guessed it was because he wanted us to hear what he had to say.

Then Father Jansen said, "I think we could all say in union, they were very kind and nice spirits. The two are flying around and sitting on top of the fireplace. It was really very entertaining when we could see them, yet they thought we could not. All of this is a miracle we have no explanation to or behind since they are still helping in raising their child. We should go and pay our respects at the garden *Evermore Beloved* where they are buried."

I watched and heard all of their conversations as did our Kasteel Vrederic spirit lovebirds. Now I thought I would finally have a very romantic night before another war ravages through my home. I wanted to hold on to my beloved and calm my interior war that was wrecking my mind, body, and soul. A sweet passionate night to remember you from the past and create a future with you, forever be mine Margriete.

CHAPTER NINE:

PROMISES KEPT

"Promises made fly time and tide and land upon the shores of the beloveds' hearts and awaken within the hearts of the promises kept."

Kasteel Vrederic family members take eternal evermore wedding vows, as promises are kept in life and in death.

As the professors of the great Leiden University in union with Catholic and Protestant clergies spoke against the witch trials, my land the Netherlands hopefully one day will become a safe haven for all accused witches. Women from all over Europe had come fleeing to this small country to weigh themselves at the witches' weighing house in Oudewater to get the weight certificate and find their freedom. The accused witches fought for their freedom as did my land. My land fought to be independent and all her citizens fought to be free.

My household members realized the most powerful weapon on this world was love. Even throughout time, the vows of a beloved and promises are kept in life and in death. The ravishing storms of the night brought lightning, thunder, and pouring rain. The sound of pouring rain hitting on the castle rooftop did not bother anyone on this night.

A two-year-old toddler slept peacefully through the stormy night as a brave soldier father and a very brave mother watched over their child even as spirits. The dark room had a lantern on, shining with a magical glow. I walked in to take a peek at my granddaughter and realized all the lanterns were turned off as the only light glowing in the room were two dancing spirit parents. I watched my daughter was dressed in a ball gown and her soldier husband was dressed in formal attire.

They saw me and Theunis said, "Jacobus will you and Margriete give away your daughter formally this time? For even death could not keep her away from me, as my vows were eternally hers. Tonight, however, I would ask you to give her to me as her parents."

I watched Margriete walk in behind me as she watched her beautiful daughter dancing with her husband in eternal bliss. The whole room was enchanted, filled with dreamlike bliss. Margriete said, "Life is nothing without true love. Forever yours has only one meaning, it is eternally yours in life or in death."

I watched an evermore mystical couple dance within an enchanted love-filled room, where I knew love proved it could live and cross even the doors of death.

Margriete continued, "We will have a beautiful wedding for our child, for I did give birth to Griet, but you gave her the eternal bliss of true love. So, we give Griet to you our son-in-law, who shall forever be like our only son. We accept both of you as our forever members of this castle. We bless Griet within your hands and give her to you completely as we are honored our daughter has found her eternally evermore beloved."

I watched Margriete cry as she had scooped up the sleeping child in her hands and kissed both of her cheeks. Little Rietje woke up kissing her grandmother back.

Kasteel Vrederic had been decorated for the wedding of the night. The flowers had come in all different colors. The castle felt like a magical land of flowers, a castle where love blossomed through the air and spread her eternal bliss of paradise. My daughter and her beloved had taken a quiet vow in the midst of a fairytale land of flowers. No jewelry was needed nor any expensive gifts as the only thing found within this wedding venue was true love.

The only participants of this wedding were our favorite uncle Bertelmeeus, our spiritual seer Aunt Marinda, and our little toddler, the flower girl. It was a magical end to a story that never ended, as who said love and love stories end at death? Aunt Marinda had arranged for all the flowers. I hugged her and gave her a kiss on her head.

She told me, "This seer knows our land will find her independence. This land will also be known as the haven of flowers. We will be gifted some bulbs from a foreign land and then this gift will become our flower haven. I see fields after fields decorated with flowers that look to me as carpets of amazing colorful flowers."

She looked at the amazing Kasteel Vrederic and said, "Bertelmeeus and I just tried to recreate my vison. We must be happy with this flower haven for now and enjoy it. For I believe in the future, the future generations of this land will spread love around the globe through flowers."

I watched an amazing woman, and it was as if I too could see the flower haven of the Netherlands in my awakening dreams. I watched my child take her vows in the midst of this magical carpet of flowers.

Griet said, "Forever yours even in death, for even death could not separate me from you, my eternally beloved. For my vows were, I shall never let you go, neither in life nor in death. I fear nothing as you are my beloved ever after. I promise to be your eternally evermore beloved, I shall never let you go."

Theunis said, "United throughout life and in death, as there is no death to true love since our union is the beginning of many more love stories yet to be born. People are born to unite with their beloved twin flame, yet here we have died to stay united within the arms of our twin flame.

Forever yours I am as eternally evermore beloved, I shall never let you go."

He kissed his wife as Margriete and I carried our little Rietje into her sleeping chamber. Rietje said, "I love weddings. Now Opa and Oma must marry and then little Rietje will have to find for herself a man and marry him."

I saw Margriete break into a laugh and say, "Maybe soon. For now, this Oma and Opa want to have you all to ourselves."

She watched Margriete and said, "I love Opa and Oma too much! I can't marry for I shall never let Opa or Oma go, for is it not true both of your hearts beat little Rietje?"

I watched my two Margrietes as I held on to them and told both, "Forever in life or in death, my heart only beats for you."

The little one fell asleep in her Oma's embrace as the elder one watched me with her ever-loving eyes of a beloved, mesmerizing my entire being. The storm outside was dancing like a wild dancer. Even Mother Nature knew in Kasteel Vrederic tonight there were eternal lovers dancing. I held on to my wife as we had our own dance story to write through a very wild and stormy night.

I asked her, "Does the storm not bother you tonight my love?"

She said, "The only storm that is ravishing inside my mind, body, and soul is our musical dance through this wild and passionate night."

She looked directly into my eyes and said, "Jacobus promise me tonight, eternally you shall never let me go, not in life nor in death. For within your embrace, I want to spend my evermore living days and the days eternally beyond life."

I did make my promise as I told her, "Remember our promises, if only you were mine, yet tonight and forever you are mine, in life or in death, so my beloved I shall never let you go. On Earth or beyond, I only ask my Lord to give us all the hardships of life but to never separate us in life or even in death."

We had a very calm and romantic night even while the world outside had a very bumpy and stormy night. Kasteel Vrederic had today been decorated for yet another magical wedding. A Catholic priest, a Protestant pastor, a

Catholic nun, an honorable knight, and a spiritual seer had all arrived to witness a magical night at Kasteel Vrederic.

Bertelmeeus, the evergreen bachelor, had made sure his beloved Margriete gets a wedding all shall remember and keep in their records throughout time. For not having an open recorded wedding, Margriete was not accepted by my father, the previous owner of Kasteel Vrederic, even though the wedding was recorded within the souls of we the beloveds.

I watched a magnificently beautiful woman dressed in a very simple white gown, embroidered with forget-me-nots, come walking into the family parlor. A very simple wedding for a majestically beautiful and elegant woman the world had given birth to, only for me. Our granddaughter had brought in her woven basket, our favorite flowers known to the world as forget-me-nots.

Our children had been there very physically at least to our eyes, renewing the faith that love never dies. We had renewed our vows as we promised one another our mind, body, and soul on Earth and beyond. As twin flames, we shall always be together rising only for one another. I recited a poem I had written for my beloved wife.

<u>ONLY YOU</u>

Wherever my eyes travel,

They search for only you.

The moon glows to glorify you my love.

After a passionate night,

Dawn sings happy tunes only for my sweetheart.

Musical rain showers this Earth,

Giving another concert for my darling.

Chilly shivering nights,

Are nothing when I have you my flame,

For only you.

Today my love,

Today my life,

Today my beloved,

Accept my enchanting love.

For today with this eternal vow,

I accept you as my eternal twin flame.

For with this vow,

We are tied eternally.

Through the promise of immortal love,

Forever be mine,

For you were born for only me,

As I was born for

ONLY YOU.

I said, "With this poem as my vow, I only ask Margriete forever to be mine. May your name be conjoined with my name, so forever may you be known as mine. Like I had asked you, if only you were mine, I shall never let you go. With this vow you are mine throughout time."

My beautiful wife only cried as she said, "I take the vow today to be yours throughout life and even after death, for I am yours and you are mine, eternally. With this vow, I take your name as my name throughout time for eternity. May our united vows glow from this magical place, to all true lovers throughout time. May Kasteel Vrederic be known throughout time as the lover's lantern. Like a lighthouse for all lovers, Kasteel Vrederic shall be the hope and guiding light of love. May this home glow like a guiding lantern for all lovers. May Kasteel Vrederic be known as the Lover's Lighthouse, a haven for true love."

I kissed my beloved as we both watched a very loving spirit couple was on their way to make sure Margriete's wish would become a reality. We all watched the Kasteel Vrederic dome was converted into the shape of a lighthouse. There inside the visible tower room, all could see a magical lantern was placed.

Time had passed by us yet Kasteel Vrederic became known as the Lover's Lighthouse, where true love blossoms. People came from far and near as all believed hidden in the air, the waters, and the flowers of Kasteel Vrederic was the eternal bliss for true lovers. People would even gossip they would be stopped by a very ghostly looking soldier who would ask, "Who enters my daughter's home? Say are you a foe or a friend?"

No one dared to enter Kasteel Vrederic with any bad intention as then they would be burned by the inner fear of themselves and they would be cursed. Life at the beloved castle became normal yet the rumors of a haunted castle never left the home. Always throughout the days or even in the middle of the nights, people would see a soldier riding a horse through the properties of Kasteel Vrederic.

A woman had sat in front of our home for three days and three nights. When I had accompanied Margriete to the gate, she had asked the woman, "Dear woman, why do you wait here? I have tried to talk with you, but I see you hide in the woods, or under the river under the bridge of the castle gate. Please advise how could I help you?"

She then replied, "I was accused of being a witch, but I have gotten my certificate as I had landed here and asked the soldier who guards this castle at night. He had helped me. I found my freedom as I was guided within my dreams by him."

She cried for a while, then said, "Now I come back again asking for help as my children and I are hungry. Because of the war and because I was accused of witchery, I have no work. No one hires us so we go hungry. I wish the soldier or the woman with the basket can help us."

I walked back inside our property with my beautiful kindhearted wife as she called on Theunis.

Margriete asked, "Did you hear the woman outside? You had helped her before. Now she is hungry and I pray people do not go hungry. It hurts me. What can I do Theunis?"

He told us to watch as we saw our daughter Griet had carried her baskets filled with fresh baked bread, fresh churned butter, and milk. She left them at the site the poor woman was sitting.

I was not shocked at how this miracle had happened as I knew my daughter, the wartime baker who had baked fresh bread for all innocent victims. She had continued baking bread for all the needy, be it if they were the

Spaniards, or the Dutch resistance fighters, or a citizen who was hungry.

Griet had sent her bread to women who were spending the rest of their days in the abbeys, churches, or shelters. It became known to all that one just could stand near Kasteel Vrederic at any hour of the day and smell fresh baked bread. The smell had spread love through the air like magic, for even when a person had come with anger and resentment toward our castle, they had left with peace wrapped in the warm smells of fresh baked bread.

Kasteel Vrederic had found visitors from far and near wishing to see the Lover's Lighthouse. It mattered not if they believed or did not, they wanted to feel the love of the Lover's Lighthouse. This lighthouse was created from love for all eternal lovers.

As for my love story, it never ended, for how could a love story end? Did our spirit lovebirds not teach all, love dies not even in death as love is immortal? Don't forget the magical phrase that had brought my beloved back within my arms. The same magical phrase had tied my daughter immortally to her eternally beloved, through life and even after death.

You can create this eternal love story with your true eternally evermore beloved. Remember to believe in the word love, and your beloved eternal twin flame. Believe in your eternal union and call upon one another from your soul. Twin flames will fly toward one another through life or even crossing the doors of death.

To mark your love story immortal, throughout time, all you must say is, "Eternally beloved, evermore beloved, I shall never let you go."

Believe and utter the words while you stand and watch the lantern burn in the Lover's Lighthouse.

CONCLUSION:

ETERNALLY EVERMORE BELOVED

"Twin flames create their love stories in Heaven. As they descend upon Earth, they rekindle and light their eternal flames for one another. Never fearing death, they stay immortal through their eternal flames."

*Kasteel Vrederic is the Lover's Lighthouse, where Sir
Alexander van der Bijl and Margriete "Rietje" Jacobus
Peters make a wish and begin their journey.*

T he 14th of December 1612. A cold chilly day at Kasteel Vrederic. Today I, Jacobus van Vrederic, have written my last entry. For today, I give my two diaries to a very special girl. I had throughout the years kept my diaries. One I had called, *Eternally Beloved: I Shall Never Let You Go*.

The second one I called, *Evermore Beloved: I Shall Never Let You Go*. I had kept these two diaries within my heart as my beloved love story had found life through the pages of these enchanting passionate diaries. Today, however, I would like to pass on my diaries to my beloved granddaughter who still says, "Opa's heart beats Rietje."

Yes, my heart beats her name as it also beats for her mother, my daughter, and the beloved beholder of my mind, body, and soul, my wife. So, today I would like to gift my beloved granddaughter the story of how a very powerful woman had taken all of my mind, body, and soul and made we the two into we the one. This magical love story is the key to our Lover's Lighthouse, which glows still as the lantern is magically lit at dusk. I give the pages that have bound our love story, into the loving hands and care of my beloved granddaughter, my little Rietje.

A young twenty-year-old woman still runs and chases her very old ninety-year-old great-uncle Bertelmeeus, as he too had not let her go, as he had promised. I watched my granddaughter as I had left my diaries on her bedside table. I knew as dusk arrives in the skies above Kasteel Vrederic, today referred to as Lover's Lighthouse, the magical lantern will guide my granddaughter to the diaries.

My beloved wife Margriete had lit a lantern on top of her bedside table to guide our granddaughter to the diaries. I left a loving letter for her to keep the promises going. Always at dusk, my beloved wife and my spirit daughter make sure all the lanterns are lit in Kasteel Vrederic. I hope my diaries will be the glowing light of hope guiding my granddaughter from which she will learn the true meaning of infinite love and its significance. I left a letter hidden in my diaries for my beloved granddaughter, whom I shall never let go from my internal soul.

14th of December 1612

Dear Rietje,

Today you are a beautiful, loving young woman, the heartbeats of Opa and Oma, and the love and joy of your brave father and your very courageous mother. I would want you to open and read these diaries as they will show how you, with your very tiny hands and little footsteps, had carved and given feelings to a man who believed he was made out of a stone. Your arrival had shown me it was alright to cry and let out the tears which I had stored in my emotionless self.

You shall see how before you, your mother had shown it is not just in life but even after death, the love stories continue. You will find out how your beloved Oma had won my heart within days of her arrival. All of these stories are still found as you still receive the hand-woven baskets filled with fresh baked warm bread from your mother.

Remember my dear, to always listen to your heartbeats as they will always guide you upon the right path, a path I will always flower with forget-me-nots. Through the dark stormy nights, this Opa shall always light a lantern for you to be guided by. Through the starlit skies, I will send you my blessings and all my love.

Always through the good and bad days or nights, you shall have the heartbeats of this Opa singing to you through the winds,

the pouring rains, and the ever-
bright sunlit days or the glowing
moonlit nights. Never fear the
outrageous fury of Mother Nature
as I will be there always
blanketing you from all the
dangers of life.

Forever remember, this Opa's
heart beats Rietje's name. So, this
heartbeat shall always guide you
to all of the blessings of this life.
Remember my child, when you
find your true beloved, you too
shall say to make your love story
immortal, "I shall never let you

go."

Keep this letter safely in the diary for with this letter, I mark my last entry. May you begin a diary and mark tomorrow as your first entry. Create your own story through only your eyes as you write for you and your entranced beloved.

Always say all your thoughts in front of the Lover's Lighthouse as the lantern is being lit. Remember the lantern was created through the spellbinding love of my beloved daughter and her beloved husband. This enchanted Kasteel Vrederic, everyone now knows as the Lover's Lighthouse. Remember my precious child, when you do find him, do not wait to say, "If only you were mine," but say, "Entranced beloved, I shall never let you go."

With all my love,

Your beloved Opa,

Jacobus van Vrederic

(Yes, my heart beats Rietje.)

15th of December 1612,

In the front gardens of

Kasteel Vrederic,

Naarden, the Netherlands

My name is Margriete "Rietje" Jacobus Peters. Today, I found this enchanted love potion-filled diary left for me by my very young and handsome Opa who is right now busy swinging on the swing with my Oma. I had made the miraculous swing with him and my great-uncle Bertelmeeus.

My Opa had written in his diaries never to end a story for a story never ends yet another one begins. So, I had tried to talk to my spirit, yes very real not see-through but very visible parents, yet invisible when they don't want me to ask them a question.

I asked them, "Papa, Mama. Can I go and join the war and try to help the soldiers? I would like to do my share, if I am allowed."

I knew they ignored me as I saw my grandparents smiling for they knew I was being ignored. I then said, "Papa, I want to look for an entranced beloved I can maybe fall in love with."

The whole Kasteel Vrederic trembled like a tremor. I then heard a loud bang and saw my soldier father standing in front of me as he said, "What did you say!"

The anger-filled voice got louder as he said again, "You want to go fishing for a suitor, in a war zone? Well young lady, you will do no such thing as long as I am still alive."

Then I saw Mama come in as she only watched Papa as he said, "Dead or alive, you will not even think of courting, do you hear me?"

My parents started to chase me as I said, "Mama, Papa, I heard you two, but I want to start my story and add it to Opa's diary."

My grandparents stood up as they held on to me and my Opa said, "Remember to write your own story. The diary is alive. All you have to do is tell her the truth, the whole truth, as then she will have your story written through words into another passionate and immortal love story, where you and your evermore beloved will recite to one another, 'I shall never let you go.'"

My Oma watched me and said, "My precious child, remember to stand in front of the Lover's Lighthouse and ask and seek whom your heart desires, if you are searching for your infinite twin flame. Only if your heart seeks the truth and knows the truth, and if the person standing by you is your beloved, then you both will see a couple appear in the lighthouse as this was your parents' unconditional gift of love left for you. This my dear is also my blessing left eternally for all true lovers as my daughter and her beloved Theunis will guard true lovers through this lighthouse for, ever after."

So, tonight I had stood in front of the Lover's Lighthouse and wished my eternally beloved finds me as I wanted to find him too. I prayed my country finds her freedom and maybe I will travel somewhere far to a fantasyland where my beloved will be waiting for me under the same skies, just maybe.

I was running impatiently as I knew my Oma wanted me to be in bed before dark. Nonetheless, I bumped into someone very hard as if he was made out of iron or steel. There in front of me was a very tall knight with a sword and his beautiful black horse by his side.

I asked him, "Who are you? Why have you entered my Kasteel Vrederic?"

He said, "I am Alexander van der Bijl, a knight and great-grandnephew of Sir Krijn van der Bijl. I was personally asked by the great knight to keep an eye on your castle, as it was a promise given by my great-granduncle to your grandfather. The protection will include you too as you are an inhabitant of this castle, I believe. If not, then I will personally escort you out of here."

As the moon shined above Kasteel Vrederic in the moonlit courtyard, I saw a very attractive man, six feet, four inches tall, with black hair and green eyes, dressed in a knight's attire. He stood in front of me and wanted to escort me out of my castle. Yet I knew I could escort him out of Kasteel Vrederic as I might be a woman but I am a trained swordswoman, as I was trained by Sir Krijn himself.

I first finished my prayers in front of the lighthouse. As he too watched me, he did the same gesture as if he too prayed. Then he watched me as I screamed, "Opa! Oma! Who is this very rude guy?"

Oh yes, the love stories within Kasteel Vrederic never end, as if you can't go and find your beloved then just maybe he will come to you. Do you believe in true love stories? I believe love stories never end as my love story begins right here. Charmed and spellbound by the first sight of a stranger, I named my diary as my beloved Opa had magically known or maybe seen, *Entranced Beloved: I Shall Never Let You Go.*

The end, no, I should say the beginning.

Signed,

Margriete "Rietje" Jacobus Peters

My Dear Readers,

I know you all are wondering what about Margriete "Rietje" Jacobus Peters, Sir Alexander van der Bijl, and their love story? Does their passionate romantic story find its way to your homes? Well, I guess you have to read Rietje's diary. Keep an eye out for the third, fourth, and fifth books in the *Kasteel Vrederic* series. Now you must cross time to the twenty-first century for Rietje's diary will reappear in the Kasteel Vrederic library in the twenty-first century. So keep reading *Be My Destiny* and *Heart Beats Your Name* first for it is only then within the Kasteel Vrederic library will reappear the fifth book in this series,

Entranced Beloved: I Shall Never Let You Go.

-Ann Marie Ruby

GLOSSARY

Get acquainted with some Dutch words, places in the Netherlands, and historical figures that were used in this book.

's-Hertogenbosch Also known as Den Bosch, municipality and capital city of the province of North Brabant

Baexem Town in the province of Limburg

Breukelen Town in the province of Utrecht

Bussum Town in the province of North Holland

Charles V Several titles including King of Spain from 1516 to 1556 and Holy Roman Emperor from 1519 to 1556, born in 1500 and died in 1558

De Heksenwaag The witches' weighing house in Oudewater

Den Haag The Hague, political capital of the Netherlands, municipality and capital city of the province of South Holland

Eindhoven	City and municipality in North Brabant
Frisia	Present-day Friesland, province in northern Netherlands
Gueldres	Former duchy in the Netherlands
Gulden	Gold coins
Helmond	City and municipality in the province of North Brabant
Het Spaanse Huis	The Spanish House in Naarden
Horn	Town in the province of Limburg
Horne	Historic county in present-day the Netherlands and Belgium
Kasteel	Castle
Kasteel Baexem	Baexem Castle in Baexem in the province of Limburg
Kasteel Duurstede	Duurstede Castle in Wijk bij Duurstede in the province of Utrecht
Kasteel Helmond	Helmond Castle in Helmond in the province of North Brabant
Kasteel Waardenburg	Waardenburg Castle in Waardenburg in the province of Gelderland

Maas	River Meuse, flows through the Netherlands, Belgium, and France
Monniksgraeve	Waterway, now known as Grote Wetering, in the province of North Brabant
Naarden	City in the province of North Holland
Oma	Grandmother
Ontbijtkoek	Dutch breakfast cake
Opa	Grandfather
Oss	City and municipality in the province of North Brabant
Oudewater	Town and municipality in the province of Utrecht
Polsbroek	Village in the province of Utrecht
Roermond	City, municipality, and diocese in the province of Limburg
Sint-Christoffelkathedraal	St. Christopher Cathedral in Roermond in the province of Limburg
Sint-Janskathedraal	St. John's Cathedral in 's-Hertogenbosch in the province of North Brabant

Terschelling Island and municipality in the province of Friesland

Tiel Town and municipality in the province of Gelderland

Utrecht Municipality and capital city of the province of Utrecht

Vught Town and municipality in the province of North Brabant

Vuurtoren Brandaris Brandaris Lighthouse in West-Terschelling in the province of Friesland

Wadden Sea Sea at the northernmost part of the Netherlands, between the Netherlands, Germany, and Denmark

Willem van Oranje William of Orange, also known as William the Silent, Founding Father of the Netherlands

Woerden City and municipality in the province of Utrecht

ABOUT THE AUTHOR

Ann Marie Ruby is an international number-one bestselling author. She has been a spiritual friend through her books. The bond between her readers and herself has been created through her books. The blessed readers around the globe have made Ann Marie's books bestsellers internationally. She has become from your love, an international number-one bestselling author.

If this world would have allowed, she would have distributed all of her books to you with her own hands as a gift and a message from a friend. She has taken pen to paper to spread peace throughout this Earth. Her sacred soul has found peace within herself as she says, "May I through my words bring peace and solace within your soul."

As many of you know, Ann Marie is also a dream psychic and a humanitarian. As a dream psychic, she has correctly predicted personal and global events. Some of these events have come true in front of us in the year 2020. She has also seen events from the past. You can read more about her journey as a dream psychic in *Spiritual Lighthouse: The Dream Diaries Of Ann Marie Ruby* which many readers have said is "the best spiritual book" they have read. As a humanitarian, she has taken pen to paper to end hate crimes within *The World Hate Crisis: Through The Eyes Of A Dream Psychic.*

To unite all race, color, and religion, following her dreams, Ann Marie has written two religiously unaffiliated prayer books, *Spiritual Songs: Letters From My Chest* and *Spiritual Songs II: Blessings From A Sacred Soul*, which people of all faiths can recite.

Ann Marie's writing style is known for making readers feel as though they have made a friend. She has written four books of original inspirational quotations which have also been compiled in one book, *Spiritual Ark: The Enchanted Journey Of Timeless Quotations.*

As a leading voice in the spiritual space, Ann Marie frequently discusses spiritual topics. As a spiritual person, she believes in soul families, reincarnation, and dreams. For this reason, she answers the unanswered questions of life surrounding birth, death, reincarnation, soulmates and twin flames, dreams, miracles, and end of time within her book *Eternal Truth: The Tunnel Of Light.* Readers have referred to this book as one of the must-read and most thought-provoking books.

The Netherlands has been a topic in various books by Ann Marie. As a dream psychic, she constantly has had dreams about this country before ever having any plan to visit the country or any previous knowledge of the contents seen within her dreams. Ann Marie's love and dreams of the Netherlands brought her to write *The Netherlands: Land Of My Dreams* which became an overnight number-one bestseller and topped international bestselling lists.

To capture not just the country but her past inhabitants, Ann Marie wrote for this country, *Everblooming: Through The Twelve Provinces Of The Netherlands*, a keepsake for all generations to come. This book also became an overnight number-one bestseller and topped international bestselling lists. Readers have called this book "the best book ever." They have asked for this book to be included in schools for all to read and cherish.

Love Letters: The Timeless Treasure is Ann Marie's thirteenth book. This book also became an overnight bestseller and topped international bestselling lists. Within this book, Ann Marie has gifted her readers fifty of her soul-touching love poems. She calls these poems, love letters. These are individual stories, individual love letters to a beloved, from a lover. In a poetic way, she writes to her twin flame. These poems are her gifts to all loving souls, all twin flames throughout time. All poems have an individual illustration retelling the stories, which Ann Marie designed herself.

Eternally Beloved: I Shall Never Let You Go is Ann Marie's fourteenth book. This is her first historical romance fiction, set within the Eighty Years' War-ravaged country, the Netherlands. You can travel through the eyes of Jacobus van Vrederic to the sixteenth century and find out how he battles time to find out love lives on even beyond time. His promise, however, is seen throughout the book and follows him to the sequel as he vows to his eternally beloved, "I shall never let you go."

Now come and step into the sixteenth century once again with Ann Marie as she presents Book Two in the *Kasteel Vrederic* series. Jacobus van Vrederic, a Dutch nobleman, returns to fight a war within a war, through the Dutch Eighty Years' War. Time is his enemy. Through his journey, he tries to rescue some innocent women from being burned at the stakes or becoming a victim at the gallows. Yet Jacobus must through this war fight his own war and find his evermore beloved. Was she too a helpless victim of the witch burnings? Find out how a gallant knight and a daring seer join the returning spirits of Kasteel Vrederic to rescue the evermore beloved of Jacobus van Vrederic, in an eternal, everlasting, emotional, and heartfelt historical romance fiction, *Evermore Beloved: I Shall Never Let You Go*.

You have her name and know she will always be there for anyone who seeks her. Ann Marie's home is Washington State, USA, yet she travels all around the world to find you, the human with humanity.

For more information about Ann Marie Ruby, any one of her books, or to read her blog posts and articles, subscribe to her website, www.annmarieruby.com.

Follow Ann Marie Ruby on social media:

Twitter: @AnnahMariahRuby

Facebook: @TheAnnMarieRuby

Instagram: @Ann_Marie_Ruby

Pinterest: @TheAnnMarieRuby

BOOKS BY THE AUTHOR

INSPIRATIONAL QUOTATIONS SERIES:

This series includes four books of original quotations and one omnibus edition.

Spiritual Travelers:
Life's Journey From The Past
To The Present
For The Future

Spiritual
Messages:
From A Bottle

Spiritual Journey:
Life's Eternal Blessings

Spiritual
Inspirations:
Sacred Words
Of Wisdom

Omnibus edition contains all four books of original quotations.

Spiritual Ark:
The Enchanted Journey Of Timeless
Quotations

SPIRITUAL SONGS SERIES:

This series includes two original spiritual prayer books.

SPIRITUAL SONGS: LETTERS FROM MY CHEST

When there was no hope, I found hope within these sacred words of prayers, I but call songs. Within this book, I have for you, 100 very sacred prayers.

SPIRITUAL SONGS II: BLESSINGS FROM A SACRED SOUL

Prayers are but the sacred doors to an individual's enlightenment. This book has 123 prayers for all humans with humanity.

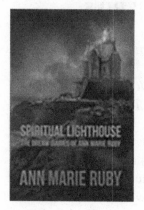

SPIRITUAL LIGHTHOUSE: THE DREAM DIARIES OF ANN MARIE RUBY

Do you believe in dreams? For within each individual dream, there is a hidden message and a miracle interlinked. Learn the spiritual, scientific, religious, and philosophical aspects of dreams. Walk with me as you travel through forty nights, through the pages of my book.

THE WORLD HATE CRISIS: THROUGH THE EYES OF A DREAM PSYCHIC

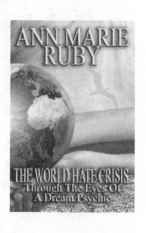

Humans have walked into an age where humanity now is being questioned as hate crimes have reached a catastrophic amount. Let us in union stop this crisis. Pick up my book and see if you too could join me in this fight.

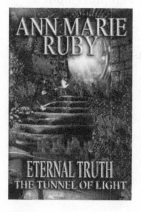

ETERNAL TRUTH: THE TUNNEL OF LIGHT

Within this book, travel with me through the doors of birth, death, reincarnation, true soulmates and twin flames, dreams, miracles, and the end of time.

THE NETHERLANDS: LAND OF MY DREAMS

Oh the sacred travelers, be like the mystical river and journey through this blessed land through my book. Be the flying bird of wisdom and learn about a land I call, Heaven on Earth.

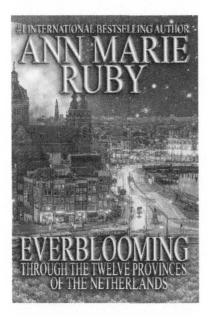

EVERBLOOMING: THROUGH THE TWELVE PROVINCES OF THE NETHERLANDS

Original poetry and hand-picked tales are bound together in this keepsake book. Come travel with me as I take you through the lives of the Dutch past.

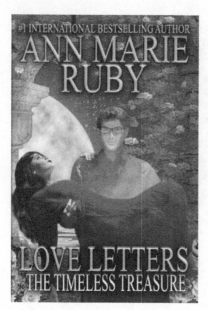

LOVE LETTERS: THE TIMELESS TREASURE

Fifty original timeless treasured love poems are presented with individual illustrations describing each poem.

KASTEEL VREDERIC SERIES:

ETERNALLY BELOVED: I SHALL NEVER LET YOU GO

Travel time to the sixteenth century where Jacobus van Vrederic, a beloved lover and father, surmounts time and tide to find the vanished love of his life. On his pursuit, Jacobus discovers secrets that will alter his life evermore. He travels through the Eighty Years' War-ravaged country, the Netherlands as he takes the vow, even if separated by a breath, "Eternally beloved, I shall never let you go."

EVERMORE BELOVED: I SHALL NEVER LET YOU GO

Jacobus van Vrederic returns with the devoted spirits of Kasteel Vrederic. A knight and a seer also join him on a quest to find his lost evermore beloved. They journey through a war-ravaged country, the Netherlands, to stop another war which was brewing silently in his land, called the witch hunts. Time was his enemy as he must defeat time and tide to find his evermore beloved wife alive.

Coming Soon

**BE MY DESTINY:
VOWS FROM THE
BEYOND**

**BE MY DESTINY:
VOWS FROM THE BEYOND**

The third book in this series is
coming soon.

**HEART BEATS
YOUR NAME:
VOWS FROM THE BEYOND**

The fourth book in this series is
coming soon.

Coming Soon

**HEART BEATS
YOUR NAME:
VOWS FROM THE
BEYOND**

Coming Soon

**ENTRANCED
BELOVED:
I SHALL NEVER LET
YOU GO**

**ENTRANCED BELOVED:
I SHALL NEVER LET YOU
GO**

The fifth book in this series is
coming soon.

Made in the USA
Las Vegas, NV
28 December 2023

83649539R00121